COCO WAS PARADISE

GARY BRUN

Book design and production by Fontaine Publishing Group

First Printing, 2019

ISBN: 978-0-6486527-0-0

www.garybrunwrites.com / IG: garybrunwrites

Thank you to everyone who made this project possible through the crowd-funding campaign.

Without you, this doesn't exist.

To my uncle.

1

If you want to know what I've been doing or where I've been, I should probably begin telling my story from the start. Although this isn't the literal start of the story, that'd be too boring, rather it's the start of the story where things began unraveling for me—at a faster rate than they had been before, at least. Yet before I start that story, I'd better fill you in on a few details that got me to that beginning, that more precarious Act One.

I'd been in Spain a short time, a few weeks maybe, it was sometime in late May 2008 when I'd arrived, and I'd spent most my time bumping around bars and cafes, not doing a hell of a lot other than guzzling down gallons of booze with strangers whose language I couldn't speak or understand. It was the kind of trip without any direction or narrative to tie it down, trading lovers and cities like baseball cards, a rambling odyssey designed to inspire something in me, but to be perfectly honest I was lacking the right kind of eyes to be inspired.

Rather my eyes were tired and heavy, barely supported by ever darkening circles and overshadowed by an even darker brow. During the morning hours my eyes were always half closed, fighting off the light which antagonised the permanent hangover which I had made my home, and in the afternoon, around 1 or 2 p.m. when the sun was at its most vibrant and most Spanish, they'd widen and begin to sparkle a little. A tenacity would burn in them as I would quit one bar for another — again and again and again. In the evening they were electric and alive and perhaps even a little scary, and that was me in my element. My truest self. Like a hunter stalking wild cats in the deepest, darkest jungle, I would prowl the bars and taverns of the city looking for an exclamation mark to put my night out of its misery, at which point I'd pass out in order for the cycle to begin again. None of those eyes were looking for inspiration, though, they were only ever looking for that next drink, which was never far away and never helpful.

I should warn you, I suppose, in this story there are bars and drinks in nearly every paragraph, so if that isn't what interests you, reader, perhaps you should put this book down and look someplace else on the shelf. There's bound to be a better book in reach, one more suited to your tastes. But if you like drinks and bars and summers in northern Spain and fabled love stories, then this might entertain you for at least a while, maybe for an afternoon by the sea somewhere with your own drink within reach, and perhaps you'll even make it to the end to discover just how I got to where I am right now, on a sailing boat somewhere, lost under the stars, writing my story in a tattered blue notebook because there's not a hell of a lot else to do out here.

Other things to note: I'm an Australian and I have family in Spain who I'd been avoiding as I didn't like who I'd become. I was also escaping a broken relationship and a sad family history and a complete absence of any goals or ambition. It should also be noted that around this time in Spain there was a violent terrorist movement (a political movement Emilio would call it), from a group named ETA (*Euskadi Ta Askatasuna*), who were fighting for the freedom of the Basque Country and blowing up a lot of innocent people in the process. That's enough for now, I think, but if there's anything I've left out you can probably track down my email easy enough and I'll answer your questions, if I ever get off this damn boat and publish this thing. As for the story I want to tell, well it starts with a girl named Coco (maybe not her real name), and it begins in a bar—like all good stories do.

Well, if you like those kinds of stories, I mean.

* * *

It was a wooden bar, an old bar, a traditional bar I suppose you'd call it, with antique fishing equipment and paintings of Moby Dick on the walls and nets hanging from the ceiling. A bar with bites of food, known as *pintxos* here in San Sebastian, prepped and served on the counter and only one tap for beer and no windows—just a door. A long bar, a narrow bar—definitely not a wide bar. A bar with tiled floors and copper ceiling fans and waiters shouting down one another in the Basque language. A bar with fishermen, real fishermen, tough and worn-out fishermen, faces long and smashed-up like peanut shells crushed underfoot, with salty skin and glares like wounded sharks. A regular bar in this part of Spain, a bar with character. I'm sure the bar had a name, but I'd never remember it, it isn't important, it was just a bar, a regular bar, and on this afternoon, outside the bar, it stormed. Not a regular storm, though, a big storm, and for the sake of the story let's pretend the storm was even bigger than it was, so it was a really, really big storm.

Tides of rain swept people off the streets and dumped them indoors like fish tossed into tepid rock-pools. They were the kind of people who wouldn't normally be in a bar like this at this time of day, but thanks to the strength of the rain and the wind they had little choice but to take advantage of the shelter. I stood at the bar alone with a drink, as I rarely sat at tables in Spain, preferring instead to remain on my feet and watch the pantomime of waiters—old and grey with black vests and bowties and resolute brows and bristling moustaches—bickering with one another and shouting over restless seas of customers to take orders from the back of the room. I looked around and followed the commotion with a rising interest. The people who came in off the street were drenched to the skin, to the point where an arm's length of barnacles wouldn't have looked astray, and they shared the same look of horror on their faces. I finished my beer and ordered another. It was now becoming overcrowded and uncomfortable, and I was beginning to think I didn't like it here anymore, the bar had changed. In all the commotion the fishermen had sailed out, fearing neither wind nor rain, and in turn the tourists had taken their places. It was as if the seasons were switching before my very eyes. I became agitated, I started drinking my beer quicker as I wanted to get out of there now. There were other bars nearby, almost every second doorway was a bar in the old town of San Sebastian, and I figured there'd probably be a few at least that were spared this intrusion of the tourist classes.

I turned back to the bar and struggled for the attention of the waiter in order to fix my cheque, when an arm brushed up against my own, slow and gentle and almost intimate. It was a life-changing arm for me, soft-skinned and cold and wet with a slight tint to it which betrayed a fair complexion, while my own was warm and dry and deeply suntanned, the black hairs long before bleached blonde by the sun. 'I'm sorry,' the owner of the arm said as she pulled it away, wiping herself dry. 'It's no problem,' I replied. This is the real start of the story I want to tell, the beginning of my own Act One.

I liked the bar again. The waiter brought the

cheque over, only four euros for five beers, and I told him not to bother, I had changed my mind and I was planning on having at least a few more. It'd been a lonely day for me, which at this point in the trip had been pretty much the norm, spent trying to find the right atmosphere to fit my mood until my mood had been smashed senseless by all the drinks. In fact, there was no recognisable mood anymore, just a dopey haze of regret. The owner of the arm ordered a beer in better Spanish than my own and turned to me and smiled, at least in my memory she smiled, and so I smiled back. I raised my glass to her: 'salud!'

'What's your name?' she asked.

'My name's …'

Suddenly a deafening crack tore the room apart and drenched the bar with a violent wave of silver light. Everyone shrieked and dropped to the floor as a unit. It was as if an explosion had been set off right outside the door, which had become pretty common in these parts of Spain of late. Everyone remained still and disorientated for a few moments longer until the realisation set in that it was just a combination of lightning and thunder, presumably right on top of us, rather than a bomb set off by ETA. I got up from the floor and squeezed my way through the space and took a look out the glass doors. The storm was picking up, no longer was it just a downpour, it looked as if a cyclone was forming, as black and purple clouds spun around one another like partners in an ill-rehearsed tango. I returned to my place at the bar where the girl was still climbing to her feet. I put out my hand to help her.

'Everything's swirling around out there,' I said, 'looks like it's gonna be a real rough night.'

'It's a nautilus spiral,' she said, shrugging her shoulders as if she knew all there was to know. 'It's in everything in nature, the way a hawk circles its prey, a cyclone, a seashell.' She lifted up her ponytail, it was yellow-gold like the faded terracotta on a bombed-out villa—which can be found everywhere in Spain, permanent reminders of a merciless civil war—to reveal a tattoo. It was a line that spun around itself in a circular motion, a nautilus spiral I supposed, 'and it's also on me, I'm also nature,' she laughed as her eyes lit up like searchlights at sea.

'So, where are you from?' I asked, yelling over the rain. The place had descended into chaos, the explosion of lightening having jolted everyone into a 'happy to be alive' camaraderie. They flooded towards the bar now, eager to drink.

'Guess,' she shouted back, grinning.

'I don't want to, I hate games like that,' I replied, pinning her accent to somewhere in northern Europe, although I could barely hear a word she said.

'Then you'll never know,' she responded, raising her eyebrows in fake remorse. It was about this moment, as she stood there teasing, when it became clear to me just how beautiful my new friend was.

'It can be your secret, I guess. I don't need to know,' I told her.

'Fine, have it your way, be boring. And you, what's your secret?' she asked as I moved my eyes downwards and noticed her lips, perhaps I stared too long, but I couldn't bring myself to look away.

'I'm lonely,' I said, looking back into her eyes, 'I'm lost, I'm running out of money and it's storming outside. That a good enough secret for you?'

'You're not alone anymore,' she replied, smiling as she reached out a hand to my shoulder, 'let's have a shot together.'

We had a shot, *aguardiente* the bartender called it, and it went down like lava and she enjoyed it even less. More drinks happened as more people sought out sanctuary in the much abused bar, and the girl and I flirted with the meaning of our meeting.

'Why are you in Spain?' I asked.

'To meet you, I guess.'

'This is gonna be a disappointing trip if that's the truth.'

'Oh, come on, you don't look too bad. A little scruffy maybe.'

She wasn't wrong, I was scruffy, I'd stopped worrying about my appearance weeks earlier.

'But why, really?' I continued.

'Well I've got to be somewhere, haven't I?'

I took a mental note—she didn't want me to know, she didn't want me to know anything.

'And you, why are you here?' she asked.

'I needed to get away, besides, I've gotta be somewhere too, right?'

'And you had to meet me!' she chimed in.

'And I had to meet you,' I agreed.

By now the bar was beyond full and the chaos wasn't fun anymore, I wanted to be alone with her, away from here. Everything was suddenly irritating, everything that wasn't her.

'You wanna get outta here?' I asked, reaching for my wallet to pay the cheque.

'But it's still raining, we'll get so wet.'

'Not if we run, there's a decent place around the corner, real close. Besides, why are you afraid of a little water?'

'I'm not afraid,' she responded, her face turning serious for the first time since I'd met her. 'Just so you know, I'm not afraid of anything.'

We finished our beers, paid the cheque and pushed through the crowd before stumbling out onto the cobblestoned streets. I knew the town well enough, having been there several times before, and led her through the narrow avenues, taking every opportunity to stay dry under the too few awnings. At one point we were out of options and she pulled me into a doorway. We were pressed closely together.

'Where's this mysterious bar?' she asked.

'It's back there but it looked too packed. There's one more place but the music is terrible. Really fucking terrible.'

'Maybe I'll like it.'

'If you do, I'll have to leave you.'

'You'd never leave me,' she laughed, 'don't even kid yourself that you could ever leave me.'

I held her hand tight and led her across the street. We burst into the bar and everyone turned, holding back a laugh as they took in our appearance, drenched explorers rising from the depths of Atlantis. The music was terrible and she loved it. She was becoming more and more beautiful now with every sideways glance, every flash of fire in her eyes, every shot of rum. We drank and danced as close as we could without ever really touching, her thin black dress swaying in the dark as her terracotta hair swept back and forth across her face like a palm frond battling a tropical typhoon. I took a step away and watched on. At one point a bearded Basque took her hand and danced with her closely, intimately even, their hips pressed firmly together, her breasts sliding up and down his torso, glistening with his sweat. She enjoyed his touch, but her eyes never stopped searching for mine. Eventually she came back to me.

'Are you always like this,' she asked, 'leaning against the wall with a drink looking bored?'

'I'm not bored at all; I just don't like dancing, but I enjoy watching you.'

'Who doesn't like dancing?'

'Me,' I smiled, taking a sip.

She shrugged me off and returned to the floor and continued shaking her hips until I gave in and joined her. Our lips were a fraction of a centimetre apart now, but we both withheld. There was more dancing and more drinks, and the music improved with each one. At some point the music got louder as the rain outside seemed to die away. I walked to the door and took a look. People were slowly returning to the street as the first rays of sunlight broke through the clouds and caressed the buildings with gentle pinks and yellows.

'The rain has stopped,' I told her as she joined me at the door, sipping on a rum and coke the bearded Basque had bought her.

'You know what'd be nice?' she asked.

'What?'

'A swim. I love to swim after a storm, the sea is so warm.'

'Easy, I know a place,' I said.

I paid the tab and we fled the bar, taking a left and then a right and then another left before charging full steam ahead to the beach.

'There are some steps over here, easy access to the sea,' I said.

We crossed along a steel-grill walkway, which jutted out over the eastern corner of Playa de la Concha like an invisible pier. At the end of the walkway was a staircase that descended down into the sea. Despite the rain having passed the area was deserted. People were making use of the moment's grace to return to their hotels or apartments or were too drunk to notice or too drunk to care. The sea was ours and ours alone. The girl slipped off her dress.

She was incredible to look at. Her eyes danced like fire but with the cold and calculating colour of reflected ice and sea and sky. She hadn't lied to me, she *was* nature. Her neck was thin and elegant and long; two hopelessly fragile shoulders, which shrugged every time she'd flirt, supported it. Her mouth, always half open, always curious, was like a child's. Her lips were a woman's lips, though, there was no doubting that, red and firm and full. There was vulnerability behind the beauty, which she was revealing to me now as a breeze chilled her naked body.

'Let's dive in,' I whispered, 'I'll race you to that boat.'

She looked up, her eyes had changed.

'I still don't know your name,' she said.

'Arthur,' I replied, 'or Artie. And yours?'

'Coco,' she said and nothing more, just 'Coco.'

'Well, it's nice to meet you Coco.'

I stripped off and beat Coco to the boat. It was a small wooden fishing boat painted blue and white but mostly blue and loaded with nets, just a regular fishing boat. For what seemed like an eternity Coco and I made love on that boat, rocking it gently on the hushed sea while the clouds and seashells did their nautilus thing but dared not bother us. The bars on the waterfront supplied a soundtrack of distant jazz while the sky went from grey to dark-grey to purple to black. We could smell sardines cooking on open fires in restaurants nearby and occasionally a bird would come and perch close to us, watching everything and understanding nothing. No other eyes though, not even our own, they were closed in concrete paradise.

That's the word, isn't it.

Paradise.

2

I woke up to a blinding light, the kind of light that reveals nothing and disorientates the viewer with a wash of pulsating otherness. I shut my eyes and turned away, but the light still shone through just as fiercely. I could hear some voices above me, several of them, although I couldn't understand what they were saying or even what language they were speaking, I guessed it was either Spanish or Italian or something else, Portuguese perhaps, something foreign to me. My body was pinned down at every axis, I couldn't shift or move anything other than my neck, and even then only just. I could feel something or someone stabbing me in several places, not the impassioned thrusting of a knife but rather the sinister piercing of a needle. I tried again to look, building up the courage to open my eyes, but the light burnt my retinas like the midday sun. I persisted with a squint and could just make out some movements, by four or more people perhaps, their hands cutting back and forth like shadow puppets in a child's nightmare. They continued speaking something I didn't understand, some kind of witch-craft I imagined, as the piercings sunk deeper and the pain erupted, pulsating right through me, tormenting my limbs and the innermost parts of my skull. I went to scream and immediately all went black. I retreated into the dark, almost glad and entirely afraid.

Sometime later, days, weeks, months, who could say, I woke up again. The light was soft this time, more like a setting sun, with reds and oranges overwhelming the vibrant yellows to the point that it was almost calm. The room was silent and empty, no more puppets dancing above me, no more witchcraft. I couldn't feel anything this time, but I could notice there was something covering my mouth and nose, a plastic mask I figured, helping me to breath. I began to realise that I was probably in a hospital, receiving treatment for something I didn't know I had. I was too tired to try and work it out and so I allowed myself to fall into a deep and calming sleep as the auburn sun set around me.

The next time I woke up I was screaming loudly, and I remember there was hectic commotion all around. Hands gripped me, held me flat, I couldn't feel my legs. I couldn't feel anything except pain. Someone brought a syringe of purple liquid over; it was injected into a tube in my arm. I stopped screaming at once and I floated into nothingness. I disappeared.

Then I just woke up and I felt ok. I couldn't explain

it, I'll never be able to explain it, it just was what it was. I was uncomfortable for sure, but not in pain, not that I could notice anyway. I looked around, my legs were suspended in the air, both heavily plastered. My arms had several tubes coming in and out of them and my chest, clean shaven, was covered in little circular stickers with wires attached. The breathing apparatus seemed to be gone but I was surrounded by other machines, about six or so, keeping me alive. My hands were taped up tightly and I was unable to move my fingers more than just a little. There was a figure at the end of the bed, he was tall and dark and wore a grey jacket over a loose-fitting linen shirt. He waited a few moments before he spoke to me. His voice was smooth like velvet.

'Do you recognise me?'

I went to respond but nothing came out. I tried again and managed just a whisper, so small it must have been impossible to hear. It was as if my voice-box had been torn from my throat, which for all I knew it had.

'Come closer,' I murmured, just loud enough this time.

He came into the light. He had a weathered face, but not from working hard, from something different, from nights spent doing anything and everything but sleeping. It was handsome though, he had always been handsome. His eyes were long and thin and smiled from under his dense, black eyebrows. His hair was grey-black, and his mouth curled slightly to the right. He looked about fifty. I recognised him alright.

'Uncle Tito,' I whispered, 'Tio Tito. Why are you here? Why am I here?'

'I'll have to bring the doctor,' he replied, 'I'll be right back.' He reassured me with a kiss on the forehead and he left the room. Almost immediately I returned to sleep and dreamt of nothing but a dark blue sea and when I woke up there were now three people standing around the bed, my uncle and two others. I had a dull headache which was becoming more unbearable with every waking second.

'Good afternoon,' the woman said, 'I am Doctor Rodriguez and this is Emilio, the nurse who'll be looking after you from now on.' She gestured towards a short, round man, his head balding everywhere except at the sides, with an exaggerated nose and warm bulging eyes peering out from under giant bushy eyebrows. He looked like a cartoon.

'It's the afternoon?' I asked.

'More or less,' Dr. Rodriguez replied, 'it will be evening soon.'

'And what happened to me?'

'I was hoping you'd be able to tell me,' the doctor answered, 'but first I have to ask some questions.' Her voice was formal and precise but her accent wasn't Basque. More likely she was from Madrid. It was not dissimilar to my uncle's accent and he was from Madrid. She was taking notes while the nurse, Emilio, took his own and checked the equipment.

'What's your name?' she asked.

'You don't know my name?'

'We do, of course, but we need to check if you remember it yourself.'

'Why would I not know my name?'

'Can you answer the question or not?'

'Yes, my name is Arthur. Arthur Washington.'

'How old are you, Arthur?'

'28.'

'And where are you from?'

'Sydney.'

'Do you know your address?'

'I don't have an address.'

'What do you mean you don't have an address?'

'I moved out of my house a few months ago, after my girlfriend dumped me. I was sleeping on a friend's couch for a while. I never knew his address though as it wasn't really important at the time.'

My head was beginning to throb now, the pain was returning hard and fast and her questions were annoying me. All I wanted was to stand up, get dressed and find a bar, I was agonising for a bar.

'Sorry doctor, but my head is in a lot of pain, can we do this later?'

She smiled sympathetically and shook her head.

'I'm sorry, Arthur, but you've just regained full consciousness after a serious accident. It's important we answer these questions now. It will let us know the extent of the damage.' She shifted on her feet uneasily. 'Emilio will get you some pain medication.'

Before Emilio could leave, my uncle Tito intervened, raising his hand to block the nurse's path. Despite both being obviously Spanish, these two men could not be more genetically opposite. My uncle looked like a Greek God, which had made him a very tidy sum of money in the film industry, while the nurse, Emilio, looked like a Shakespearean fool.

'Let me go, I'll speak to the doctor at reception; I think it's best Emilio watches on,' Tito said to the doctor.

'As you please,' she responded as he left the room. 'Now Arthur,' she continued, 'did you recognise that man just now?' She raised an eyebrow, as if she thought her question was going to catch me out, which was exactly what she wanted. There was something about the doctor's tone which was beginning to really irritate me.

'Of course I recognise him, he's my uncle Tito, why?'

'Do you know what country you're in?'

'I'm in Spain, well I must be, but when I woke up the other times, I had no idea. I could've been anywhere.'

'How many other times do you remember waking up?'

'Three, maybe four.' She was writing all this down.

'Do you remember why you're in Spain?'

I thought for a moment and gave the only answer I could. 'I can't answer that question, doctor. It's impossible.'

'Why is it impossible?' she stopped writing.

'Because there is no 'why'. I came because I could, because I'd been here before, because family could bail me out if I needed it, like now, because I wanted to go hiking, I wanted to drink, I wanted the sea. I wanted to escape.'

'That sounds like reason enough to me. To escape.'

'Well if you need to write something down then sure, that'll have to do. I'm here to escape. Won't be so easy now,' I muttered, staring at my shattered legs, hung high above in ivory-coloured casts.

'From what though, may I ask? Escape from what?'

At this point Tito returned with some water and pills, and the interrogation paused as I did my best to swallow them, Tito helping prop me up on the pillow. I closed my eyes for several minutes until the drugs kicked in.

'I know this is difficult for you right now, Arthur, but I just have a few more questions.' I nodded for her to continue but my eyes remained closed. 'What do you remember about the walk you were on?'

It took me a moment to understand the question. What did she mean by walk? Then it dawned on me quite suddenly.

'You mean the Camino?'

'Yes, I suppose, if it was the Camino.'

'It was, the northern one. I remember that I was going to do it, at least a part of it, a few weeks and maybe more. I remember buying shoes for it, at a store in town, and some rain gear. I remember getting dressed one morning to leave, and then—' I paused.

'And then?' the doctor pressed.

'Nothing. That's the only memory I have, getting ready to leave.'

'Nothing else?'

'Nothing at all.'

I opened my eyes at last and turned to my uncle. 'What happened to me, Tito, why am I like this?' I needed his reassurance, I needed someone to tell me everything was fine.

He looked to the doctor and she shook her head. The colour drained from his face, it was the first time I'd ever seen him take something so seriously. It didn't suit him at all. He was the kind of man who only looked like himself with a giant grin smashed across his face and a martini in hand.

'We'll tell you soon enough, Artie,' he paused, 'but it'd be better if you could tell us.'

'What do you mean I tell you? I've already said my memory stops there.'

I stared at him blankly, I didn't know what he was trying to say. Was it even legal to keep this information from me? The doctor took Tito aside and had a conversation in Spanish, obviously I wasn't supposed to listen in.

'Artie, we'll leave it for now, and work out the best time to have this conversation later. You need to rest,' he said as he kissed my forehead once more and wished me goodnight. Then he and the doctor left together while Emilio pulled the sheets up around me.

'Thank you,' I said, 'how long have I been here?'

He looked over shoulder to see if the doctor was still there, she wasn't. 'Almost three weeks,' he whispered, 'but try to sleep for now, you'll learn more in the morning.' He turned to leave.

'Wait, Emilio, it is Emilio, yeah?'

'*Sí?*'

'I remember something, maybe it's important.'

He got out his little notepad and pen. 'Go on,' he encouraged me.

'There was a girl, a girl and a boat. Her eyes were blue and so was the boat.' Emilio smiled, as if me sharing this with him had just made us friends, which I didn't mind, God knows I needed a friend.

'Was she walking the Camino with you?' he asked.

'No, I don't think so, definitely not. But she was here, in San Sebastian with me, the night before I started walking.'

'She must have made an impression, if that's your last memory,' he raised his eyebrows and winked. 'I'll leave you to dream of her tonight, but why don't you rest now, and we can talk about her more tomorrow.' He turned out the lights and left the room.

When I was alone, I remembered something else, it was her name, just two syllables both exactly the same. It was a fun name to say but probably not her real one, although maybe it was, who was I to judge.

'Her name was Coco,' I told the dark. Then I fell asleep and felt nothing at all.

3

'I can talk to my uncle, he still holds a lot of sway,' I said to Emilio as he washed my back with a warm, soapy towel, which had become something of a morning ritual for the two of us. He shook his head, the fat of his chin swaying back and forth like a boat caught in the tide.

'And how's your uncle going to convince anyone to cast a fat, ugly, pig like me in their movie?'

'Emilio, you have to stop speaking about yourself like this. There are roles for all sorts of people in film, regardless of what they look like. Think about it, have you ever watched a film where everyone was glamorous and beautiful like Marilyn Monroe and Clark Gable? What if the character is a delivery driver or a butcher, or worse yet a paedophile priest, you think they'll want just beautiful actors?'

'So you agree then? I'm a fat, ugly, pig?'

'I didn't say that,' I defended myself, 'you're putting words in my mouth.' It was true though, Emilio was anything but handsome, however there was something endearing about the way he carried himself which made him attractive in his own unique way, in the same way you can still enjoy the company of an ugly dog. And yet despite his jokes there wasn't an ounce of self-consciousness about him, he was cheerful, light on his feet and generous with his humour. I liked his company very much and he made the hospital bearable for me, fun even, at least during the moments when the pain wasn't excruciating. Everyone else I found cold and disconnected, pissed off at me for having given them cause to turn up to work, but something about Emilio made me feel like he gave a damn, even if he probably didn't. Plus he spoke fantastic English, which I figured was no fluke. Emilio laughed and brought the towel up over my face. The warmth was smothering, and I didn't fight it off.

'You're a good boy Arthur, but the fact is I'm destined to be a nurse forever. When I was a young man maybe I could have made something more of myself, but not now. Besides, I'm good at my job, and let's not forget someone needs to take care of you.' He swapped the wet towel for a dry one and wiped down my back. 'How about you? You're still a young man, what are you going to make of yourself?'

I went quiet for a moment and descended into the deep and dark recesses of my heart. 'Don't ask me that,' I said to him, 'never ask me that. Right now I just want to get out of this hospital, it feels like I've been here forever.'

In fact I'd only been properly conscious for about two weeks, and during those two weeks Emilio and I had formed something like a friendship, mainly out of necessity, but I'd like to think if I had met him randomly out in the real world it would have been the same. I doubted it though. I still had no idea what had happened to me. The doctor was insistent that I remember it myself. 'It'll be much better for all of us if you regain something of the events that led you here,' she'd say - but there was nothing. Not even Emilio would let the truth slip and I had tried more than a few times. I could tell he wanted to share it with me, but his job was too important to risk.

All of a sudden, his fat, hairy, bear hands gripped me under the arms and propped me up higher on the pillows. My legs were heavily plastered and even the slightest movement required all his strength. By the time I was properly upright his bald head was glistening with sweat, each bead racing the others as they sailed down his forehead and settled in his eyebrows.

He brought a tray over with lunch, which was the same every day, a dry *tortilla patata* served on a paper plate and lightly heated, an apple, two fistfuls of stale bread and a half carton of warm pulp-free orange juice. Just before I started eating the doctor came in with two specialists. They started speaking Spanish as they examined me, paying particular attention to my legs. They stayed a few moments longer and left together, never bothering to say hello or ask me how I felt.

'What was that about, Emilio? I wish they'd speak English when they're talking right in front of me, I know this is their country but still.'

'Unfortunately these doctors are of a generation who never thought English would be useful, although I bet they wish they had it now, the world is changing so quickly that those without it risk getting left behind.'

'They're the same age as you though, and your English is as good as any I've heard in Spain.'

'Yes, I know, but I am a thespian, Arthur, language is my weapon, my knife, my…' he paused, gesturing a swishing movement with both hands clasped together.

'Your baseball bat?'

'No!' he kept on swishing.

'Your sword?'

'Yes! Sword! That's it, language is my sword!' he declared, with a big, sloppy *W* after the *S*. I couldn't help but laugh. My first estimation of Emilio was proving to be true, he was the definitive Shakespearean Clown.

'Anyhow, what did they say?' I asked, returning the conversation to my legs.

'Well it's good news, Arthur, you can go home on Friday, assuming your uncle sorts out a suitable place for you to live.'

'That is good news, Emilio.' A smile beamed across my face, and then almost as quickly a sadness washed over me. 'But I'll miss hanging out with you.'

'I knew you liked the soapy towel,' he joked as he leant down and hugged me. His body odour was unbearable but I chose not to spoil the moment.

The following morning, at least I think it was the following morning, Tito arrived after breakfast. With the help of Emilio and the permission of the doctor he lifted me into a wheelchair and took me out into the overgrown tropical garden behind the hospital to have a coffee together. It was acknowledged that summer was late this year and the hottest days were yet to come, but on this particular morning I remember the air almost had a winter's chill to it. In the north of Spain the weather was its own master I had come to realise. I buried my hands deep into the blanket in an effort to keep warm, the coffee balancing between my plastered legs. There were not four seasons here but rather 365, and on this day, while the sun burnt bright and fiercely in Malaga and Granada and Madrid, San Sebastian suffered through a mid-winter chill.

'I'll keep trying your mother,' he said, 'I've left a message with her doctors but they never put me through to her.'

'It's ok,' I said, 'she wouldn't be able to help, she wouldn't even understand.'

'I thought as much. Also, I've printed out the emails from your friends, I'll leave them with you, and you can let me know when you'd like me to respond.'

'Thank you. How about Julia? Did she reply yet?'

'Not yet, no, nothing from your ex,' he replied, breaking eye contact as he gazed around the garden. 'Maybe the news has upset her too much, maybe she doesn't know what to say.' He straightened up a little and turned back to me, 'I do have some good news though Artie, I've managed to find an apartment for you, right by the sea and not far from my own, in fact you can see my balcony from your window so we're practically neighbours. I'll be able to keep a close eye on you,' he joked, glowing with enthusiasm.

'You're the one who needs supervision,' I replied, 'I've heard rumours about your legendary parties and chorus-lines of mistresses. I'm sure it's quite the spectacle. But that's amazing Tito, how did you manage that?'

'Oh, it was all luck actually, I didn't lift a finger. A friend of mine, a tenor in the opera, is touring Europe for the next few months and is happy to have someone in the apartment while he's away.'

'But how will I manage on my own? I'm still a cripple,' I reminded him.

'We'll make it wheelchair friendly of course, move some stuff around so you can live freely, and there's a spare room for Emilio too, so you'll have a full time carer.'

It's hard for me to describe how much this lifted my spirits, knowing Emilio would be living with me and Tito just up the road. All at once my disability and run of bad luck had a silver lining—I'd be living by the sea without a care in the world.

'There's another thing, Artie,' he said as his face turned serious, dark even. 'I have to say I was very upset to find out from the hospital that you were travelling through Spain, in my own city even. Why didn't you call me? You could've stayed with me, we could've gone on trips, and this accident wouldn't have happened.'

I could see this really cut him deep and I felt terrible

about it, but the truth was I had a hard time connecting with anyone related to my father, and I liked to pretend that that side of me didn't exist. And yet I had chosen to visit Spain several times over the years, and I stayed with Tito most of those times and enjoyed them all. Something inside of me had changed though—I wanted to be anonymous, I wanted to be free. I felt as if I were unravelling as a person back home, and some time alone in a foreign land would put the pieces back together. Maybe not in the same way but in some new way, some stronger, more durable way. Of course, I had already proven this theory to be flawed, as I'd done nothing but drink and ramble about like a fool, blowing almost all my cash in the process.

'I'm sorry, Tito, I was working through the break-up with Julia, I thought I needed to be alone, but I was wrong, clearly very wrong. I'm lucky you're here and I should have called you earlier.'

'It's ok, Artie, just never do it again,' he leant over and put his arm around me.

'How does Emilio feel now that he won't be living with his mother anymore?' I asked, diverting the conversation away from my treason.

'He still lives with his mother?'

'Yeah,' I said, 'they share the same bedroom and everything.'

Tito could only smile and shake his head. I was glad to see him smile again, I felt a lot of guilt that I'd stolen it from him, it was not a smile that ought to be stolen.

4

Friday came in a hurry and I was all set to leave. An ambulance would take me to the new apartment where the tenor would be waiting to show Emilio and me around the place. Before this, however, I was scheduled to meet with Dr. Rodriquez alone. By now she had relaxed a little and spoke to me in a more casual tone, like a human almost. She'd even taken to calling me Artie, like my uncle always did and Emilio sometimes too. I was especially excited this morning for I figured all would finally be revealed to me. I was tired of being in the dark about my 'accident'.

'Good morning, Artie,' she said as she took a seat at the end of my bed. 'You must be happy to finally leave.'

'Yeah, I am, very much so. Don't get me wrong, I actually don't mind this hospital, Emilio has made it feel like a home for me, but it'll be nice to leave and have a view of the sea.'

'I've heard about your apartment, right opposite the opera and Playa Zurriola, it's one of the best parts of town. You've done very well.'

'Yeah, I suppose I have, but it's not like I can enjoy it, is it? I won't be catching too many waves or seeing too many shows. I'll be living through the lives of others for the summer.'

'You'll make your own fun, I'm sure, or you can use it as a time to reflect of your life, on how you got to this position.'

'Sorry to sound like a broken record but how long do you think I'll be like this?'

'In the wheelchair?'

'Yeah, and with the legs all plastered up and everything else.'

'It's hard to say, Artie. Your injuries were very severe,' she said as she pulled some x-rays out of an envelope. She held one up to me. 'See here, this is your knee, your patella, on your right leg. It was completely destroyed, and we needed to reconstruct it from scratch.',

It looked like a shattered shop window after a robbery, completely unrecognisable as a knee.

She got out another. 'This here is your tibia, or your shinbone, again on your right leg. This was a compound fracture, meaning the bone pierced through the skin. We had to bind the two halves together with screws and rods, this will take the longest time to heal. Your left leg suffered a lot less—a simple fracture, which we set naturally, so it should heal in a matter of weeks.

Apart from that there were several small bones in your ankles and wrists that were fractured, but there's not a lot we can do for that. Only time can heal them. But it's your concussion and brain injury that we're most concerned about. You still have no memory after the day you left San Sebastian to begin the Camino?'

'No,' I shook my head, 'no more than the first day I regained consciousness.'

'I'd suggest when you're well enough to leave the apartment you might want return to the locations on your pilgrim's passport. No need to walk again, just drive along the same route. Sometimes going back to the scene of the crime can re-jig the memory. Maybe you'll be able to piece it together.'

'Can you hand me the passport?' I asked, 'I'd like to see it again.'

She went through my belongings on the shelf until she found it and handed it to me. It was a small white document that unfolded out into a long, blank pamphlet with a few scattered stamps. The purpose of it was to collect stamps from each town you walked through and slept in. It was a way of proving that you were indeed a pilgrim on the Camino and not just a tourist seeking cheap accommodation. The first stamp was a faded blue cockleshell, which I got in San Sebastian, and the last was a bland rectangular one from a cheap hotel in a seaside town named Castro-Urdiales. In between were five others, meaning I'd walked seven days all up and slept in seven different towns. The next town after Castro-Urdiales was to be Laredo, but I never made it there, the accident happened before I could reach it.

'So, doctor, are you going to tell me what happened. I know I fell off something, but what? How?'

'I can, if you'd like, although I know your uncle was hoping to talk to you tonight.'

'Ok, I'll wait,' I said, figuring it was obviously important for Tito to tell me himself.

'Artie, your recovery shouldn't be too difficult, at least the physical aspect of it. But it's also important for you to recover mentally. You've been through something very stressful, very painful, and it's ok if it gets too much. The hospital will provide you with psychological support and I know Emilio likes to think himself an amateur psychologist.'

'Emilio is an amateur everything, it wouldn't surprise me if he could half-fly a helicopter,' I said, making her laugh before she promptly straightened herself.

'Also I'd suggest laying off the alcohol or any other substance for a while, at least until you're ready to go outside and rejoin the world.'

'I can't promise that, doctor. It is Spain in summer, after all, it'd be a sin to not enjoy it, injured or not.'

'Storm clouds don't care if it's summer or not.'

I nodded to show I understood, but it was a false nod and she was too smart to not see through it. She got up slowly, straightened out her coat and reached out her hand for me to shake.

'Well everything's ready downstairs, the ambulance is waiting to go whenever you like. It was nice to have met you, Arthur. However, as always with this job, other circumstances would have been preferable.'

We called for Emilio, packed the pilgrim's passport away, and left.

As it turned out, Dr. Rodriguez hadn't lied at all. The apartment was indeed in the best part of town. It was on a street called Calle Salamenca, which ran parallel along the river and down to the sea. The building was sandstone, similar to the sandstone in Sydney, but the style was more classical, with boxed-in balconies on the corners and flat shallow balconies on the front, facing directly over the canal and then to the beach and the sea beyond. The morning clouds had packed their bags and journeyed out over the hills and the weather was now warm and luxurious with a blue sky as vibrant as any you're ever likely to see. The town was bustling with the energy that only the promise of a summer's evening can inspire. The promise of drinks and tapas with friends and rendezvous with old and new lovers. The promise of Spain.

The tenor's apartment was on the fourth floor, one below the top. Unfortunately, the building was too old to accommodate a lift and so the two paramedics who delivered me took my weight over their shoulders and hauled me up the four flights of stairs. Between the two of them it wasn't much effort as I had lost a lot of weight in hospital; by now I'd weigh no more than sixty-five kilograms or maybe even less. They asked me if I liked football, but their English was so poor and my Spanish near non-existent and so all I replied was '*Si, si,*' and the conversation died a miserable death. Emilio had gone ahead with the suitcases and by the time we reached the apartment he was already introducing himself to the tenor.

'You must be Arthur,' the tenor bellowed as I arrived on his floor, his stumpy little arms reaching out as he lowered himself to hug me. 'I'm Antonio Belafonte the Third. But just call me Tony, or Bello, or whatever you please. Only God can know the number of names I've had in my life.'

'Nice to meet you, Tony, and thank you very much, this has literally saved my life.'

Tony had a small tuft of black hair which stuck to his head like a sodden tissue dropped from above and a slim black moustache, fashioned like Clark Gable's but somewhat lost on a flabby and droopy face. He looked about seventy, or maybe even older, but I'm sure his lifestyle had added more than a few years to him, so he was possibly sixty-five or less. His cheeks and nose were painted red from a lifetime of booze and he smelled of cheap after-shave and even cheaper bourbon. His voice bellowed like the distress signal of a ship battling the waves.

'How about a drink?' he hollered as the walls shook around us.

'Sure, I'm dying for one' I said, catching Emilio as he glanced daggers at me.

Tony went into the kitchen to prepare the drinks while I took a look around my new home. It was lavishly decorated with high ceilings and natural light pouring in from every direction. The furniture was polished teak and clearly expensive, and every inch of available wall was taken up with oil paintings, like a Parisian Salon. It was exactly how you'd imagine the apartment of a world-famous tenor. Emilio came over to me, moving awkwardly through the maze of furniture and antiques.

'What did Dr. Rodriguez say about drinking?' he scowled, putting on the mask of the nurse and dropping that of the friend.

'That if I was going to be living with you, I'd better get good at it.'

'Artie, don't be stupid, this isn't a good start.'

'Lay off it, Emilio, it doesn't interfere with my medication so what's the problem. She thinks I'll get depressed if I'm stuck in here drinking every day, but the truth is I'll get depressed if I don't sit here drinking every day. Besides, my uncle is a serious alcoholic and he'll likely be here all the time, so what hope do I have?'

Tony returned from the kitchen with three cocktails and took a seat opposite me, Emilio remained standing, awkwardly holding his drink as if it were a dead cat. I took a sip and a feeling of warmth washed through me. The time in hospital was the longest I'd ever gone without drinking since I'd turned 15. It felt good to be home. I took another sip and almost immediately I remembered blue eyes and a blue boat.

'Your uncle…' Tony said, staring at me with an expression I couldn't quite understand. 'Your uncle…' he repeated after a moment, and then nothing, his expression no less mysterious.

'My uncle…' I responded, forcing a smile, not sure what else to say.

'His uncle…' offered Emilio, feeling left out I

suppose. Tony and I both turned to him confused; he gave us a dopey smile and nothing else.

'Your uncle…' Tony said a third time, turning back to me, 'is the finest man I've ever met.'

'Oh, yeah, he's a special guy,' I agreed.

'He's more than special. The amount of times Tito has saved my ass, connecting me with people in the industry, pulling strings to get me gigs, keeping me out of trouble. I tell you, I wouldn't be half as successful as I am today without him. So naturally when he mentioned he had a nephew in trouble who needed a place to stay, it wasn't an if but a when.'

My relationship with Tito over the years had been that of fun uncle and energetic nephew. To be honest I didn't know a lot about him as I had always been too young and self-involved to care. What I did know was that he'd been a successful film actor when he was young and after he retired he had bought into a small production company. I figured I'd make use of Tony to find out more.

'Just how powerful is my uncle?' I asked, leaning in to catch his answer.

'In what way?'

'I don't know, you said he helped you a lot, in the industry I suppose, how powerful is he in the industry?'

'Here in Spain, Tito Ramiro Ramirez is the most powerful man in film.'

'Really? I find that hard to believe, I didn't think he even made films anymore.'

'It's not about the work, it's about the connections. No one is better connected than your uncle. He has other producers, studio heads, actors, starlets and everyone in between in his pocket. How? Because he forms relationships, friendships, and he never breaks them. Instead he nurtures them, helps them grow like a palm in the desert. You know you've really fucked up if Tito Ramiro Ramirez speaks badly of you, you might as well quit the industry and take up nursing.' He turned to Emilio and offered an embarrassed smile. 'Not that there's anything wrong with nursing.'

'I knew he was well off, but he never spoke about anything like that. I thought he might have been washed up, a thing of the past, a bit of a joke even.'

'Washed up? On the one hand, maybe, because like you said he doesn't work anymore, but the film industry is like everything else in Spain, reputation is paramount. Paramount! And no one has a better reputation than Tito. Here in San Sebastian he may as well be the king, he pays for nothing, no restaurant, no bar would dare accept his cash. Of course he then leaves a generous tip in its place',

'Well, there you go, I wonder if that makes me a prince then. The Prince of San Sebastian, it has a certain ring to it, don't you think?'

I finished my drink and Tony, the perfect host with the bellowing voice, sprang to his feet and went into the kitchen to make another. Emilio hadn't touched his.

'So, maybe it's true, your uncle could make me a star,' Emilio joked, framing his face like a fifties movie queen.

'Apparently, I'm not sure how much he's exaggerating though. Maybe he owes my uncle money or something.'

'I don't think so. Every time Tito walked into the hospital ward the nurses would faint almost on cue,' he said, chuckling like a child.

Tony returned with fresh drinks for the two of us, 'So, any questions about the apartment? It's all straightforward enough I imagine. You look like a smart enough duo. Still, I've left a list in the kitchen of things you should know. Oh, look, come over here.' Tony stood up and walked to the balcony. In front of it was a telescope. Emilio navigated the wheelchair through the room, smashing my feet into every possible piece of furniture along the way.

'This is the *pièce de résistance*,' Tony said. It was polished brass on a beautiful wooden tripod and looked like it would have cost several thousand dollars. 'Since you're going to be holed up inside for what's left of the summer, I'd hate for you to miss out on all the action,' he was crouching now, looking through it. 'There is an endless array of tits and asses on that beach for you to enjoy, or if you're like me, cocks and ass. Maybe you can send them smoke signals and invite them up, although please don't light any fires in my living room. Here, take a look,' he said, gesturing for me to take the telescope.

Emilio nervously positioned my wheelchair in front of it and I took a look. He wasn't wrong, the beach was teaming with gorgeous women and the antique machine was powerful enough to see them in detail. I felt a little self-conscious though, checking out girls on a beach from a fourth-floor apartment while two older men watched on, so I started scanning the boulevard and the apartments instead. Then I saw something.

'Wait a second.' I pulled back from the eyepiece. 'Isn't that Tito's apartment?'

Tony took over from me and looked, after a moment he found it, 'Why yes, it is, well spotted. To think I've had this all these years and never noticed, I was too busy looking for cock I suppose.'

Suddenly there was a loud honk from the street below, followed by several more. 'Fuck,' Tony yelled, looking at his watch, 'my driver has been outside for twenty-five minutes. Arthur, nice to meet you, really nice, my email is written on some paper in the kitchen.' He was running around like a madman, collecting his coat, his hat, his pipe, his cabin luggage. 'If you need anything at all just write me. Nice to meet you too, Enrique.'

'Emilio!' he shouted after him.

And with that the tenor disappeared down the stairs. I'd never see him again.

'Well, a home at last eh, Enrique,' I said, finishing the second drink.

'Give me a look,' he demanded, pulling the telescope from my grip, 'I also want to search for cock.'

I laughed as Emilio took over and I wheeled myself into the kitchen. I made another drink, my third for the day, but not nearly my last. A pattern was forming which would last the entire summer.

5

Later that night the doorbell rang a little after eleven. Emilio had gone to bed an hour or so before, but I was still awake, going through the tenor's CD collection and trying to create the sense that the apartment was now my home, if only temporarily. I'd just put on Chopin's Concertos 1 & 2, which coated the night with a blanket of melancholy, which I wrapped tighter around my ruined body with every sip of wine. I'd spent the better part of the evening staring out over the sea, watching the crowds enter and eventually exit the opera, their voices, full of anticipation first and admiration after, drifting over the canal to my balcony on the summer evening breeze. Gangs of teenagers gathered around the cobalt-coloured break wall, constructed of giant granite cubes balanced on top of one another; which gave the landscape a feeling of fragile broken heartedness. The teenagers were filling half empty bottles of Coca-Cola with bottom-shelf cask-wine and passing it around to one another like a joint. They didn't know where their night was headed and they weren't in any rush to find out. Elsewhere young lovers wrestled like untrained pups on the sand, making out and making love and not caring or knowing who was watching. Loving was easy tonight, it seemed, and the consequence would have to be tomorrow's burden. It made me remember blue eyes and a blue and white boat.

I wheeled over to the door, my legs stuck out straight like a two-pronged fork, careful not to bump any items of furniture on the way. I buzzed my uncle up. There was a short conversation on the other end, which told me he wasn't alone. I unlocked the door and a few moments later Tito entered the apartment with a young brunette girl close behind him. She looked as if she was a child only yesterday.

'Artie, so good to see you,' he exclaimed as he reached down and gave me a hug. 'Sorry I couldn't come earlier, Tahina and I were held up at dinner.'

He introduced me to Tahina as we settled in the living room and I turned the music down a little. She was beautiful, no doubt, and had the aura of a van-quished dream.

'Would you like a drink?' I asked as Tito sprung to his feet. His energy seemed a little off as well; something between them wasn't quite working and I was frustrated that they'd dragged whatever it was into my night of contemplation. I'd spent all day wanting Tito to arrive but now that he had I found him an unwelcome intruder. Maybe it was just the girl.

'Let me get it, Artie, you relax. What have you got in there?'

'Your tenor mate left the place pretty well stocked. There's wine, whiskey, beer, whatever you like. I'll have a whiskey,' I said, 'neat.'

'Of course. Tahina?' Tito asked the girl. Tahina shrugged and shook her head. I gathered she didn't speak any English.

While Tito was in the kitchen I made a small effort to talk to her but she wasn't keen on getting to know me, or sharing anything about herself, and I was really wishing now that Tito had come alone. I was too tired to make any more effort than I already was. Instead of trying to talk to her I guessed at her age instead. Eighteen, nineteen? Twenty at the absolute most. I wondered what her parents thought she was doing, what they'd say if they found out she was out drinking with one of Spain's most notorious playboys. They'd probably be stoked, I figured. After all, my uncle was a very wealthy man—what's the sacrifice of a daughter's innocence for an afternoon on a super yacht?

When Tito returned Tahina whispered something to him in Spanish. He nodded and reached into his pocket and handed her a small plastic satchel, cocaine I assumed. She got up, balancing on her gigantic heels and straightening her tiny skirt, and I directed her to the bathroom. She excused herself and trotted off. That's the transaction then, I thought to myself, he keeps her nose full and she keeps him satisfied.

'Nice girl,' I said, taking a sip of whiskey.

'Who, Tahina? She's ok, a friend of a friend. Look I'd offer you some coke Artie, but I think maybe it's too soon, I mean you're on a lot of meds right? But if you want to you can have some of course, no problem at all.' His mood had changed, he didn't seem agitated anymore, but lively and vivacious. I figured he'd done a line or two himself while preparing the drinks.

'It's ok Tito, I don't do cocaine, it's not really a thing back home. I'll leave it for you.'

'Oh yeah, of course, me neither, never actually. This is a one off, it belongs to the girl, and I thought why not? It's not like we have anything in common so it couldn't hurt, right? I've had a hell of a time tonight trying to talk to her, maybe it'll open her up a little, maybe it'll save the whole evening, it's been an absolute drag so far.'

If it belonged to her then why was he carrying it? Why did she have to ask to have a line? Tito was lying to my face but I didn't really care, I was too tired to care, and besides he had information I needed.

'But look at this place,' he continued, 'isn't it something? It used to belong to a general in the fascist army during Franco's dictatorship. He was murdered just in there,' he gestured towards Emilio's room. 'You'll be a happy boy living here Artie, that I promise you, we'll just have to find you a girlfriend I suppose, I'll ask Tahina if she has any friends. Actually you wouldn't like her friends, they're cute but that's about it. Although being cute isn't nothing, a lot of women would kill to be called cute, a lot of men, too, but you probably want a girl who reads or at least *has* read. Oh, that reminds me, here,' he reached into his pocket and pulled out a folded piece of paper, 'It's an email from Julia, she replied at last, maybe you could get her to visit, patch things up? Otherwise I'm sure Tahina has some friends, smart ones maybe, I'll ask if she has any smart friends, no promises, it won't be easy meeting girls being stuck up here though, what a shame. I'll call Tony and see if there's any cute ones who live in the building, remind me to do that tomorrow, yeah?'

Throughout his entire speech he didn't stop to breath once, let alone allow me to interject. Tahina returned from the bathroom, her right nostril coated white with powder indicating she was new at this, which confirmed the drugs weren't hers.

'Hey, Artie,' Tito started up again, 'did Tony show you the telescope?' He got up from his chair. 'The number of hours I've wasted up here watching girls get changed on the beach.' He glanced to see if Tahina had heard him, but he was safe, she was too high to even know where she was. 'And just over there,' he continued, 'you can see my apartment,' he swung the telescope to the right, 'you'll be able to watch my parties from right here, Artie, you may even be able to hear them. Get you good and excited for when you're finally well enough to join. Are you sure you don't want a line?'

'I'm sure, I'm good.'

'You can have one if you like,' Tahina said out of nowhere. So she did speak English; what else was she hiding? Maybe the drugs *were* hers.

'He knows that Tahina, he doesn't have to ask,

Artie asks for nothing, got it?' Tito reproached her.

'*Si, si,*' she responded, offering me a look of insincere condolence. 'Aren't we late?' she continued in English. Tito looked at his watch.

'Shit, alright. Look, kid,' he turned his attention to me, swallowing what was left of his drink, 'I'm sorry but we've got to get going. Al Pacino is downing martinis at the Maria Cristina, and I promised I'd join him. It's been years since Pacino has been in town and he'll be royally pissed if I miss him. I'd invite you along, but you know…' he glanced at my legs.

'It's ok, Tito, I'm pretty tired anyway, I was thinking about bed before you turned up.'

Tahina got up and marched over to me, she stuck out her hand, 'It was so nice to meet you, *so, so* nice.' I shook it, awkwardly. 'I'm so sorry about what happened to you. It's so sad.' She flung her bag over her shoulder and walked to the door, ignoring the confusion on my face. 'Are we going?' she snapped at Tito, who'd snuck off into the kitchen for another line.

'One minute!' he shouted from the other room.

'I'll meet you downstairs,' Tahina said as she turned back to me, '*so, so* sorry.'

She left and I was glad, I absolutely hated her. Tito returned from the kitchen, buzzing around the place like a fly caught on a window. He composed himself and headed for the door.

'Hey, Tito, before you leave, one thing,' I stopped him.

'Anything, Artie, anything at all,' he had one foot out of the door and no real intention of coming back in.

'I need to know what happened to me, the doctor said you'd tell me tonight. It's driving me mad. I know it's probably not a good time, but a good time probably doesn't exist.'

Tito's face changed immediately; he got that serious look which I couldn't stand. He let the door close and sat on the arm of the couch. He stared at me intensely, sitting still for the first time all night, and said just one word, 'Suicide.'

The room fell silent, the street fell silent, even fucking Chopin fell silent. Silence engulfed us.

'I'm sorry, what?' I responded after God knows how long.

He wiped his nose. Crumbs of coke dribbled out onto the couch. 'Suicide Artie, you tried to kill yourself. Jumped off a cliff ten kilometres outside of Laredo. You were lucky to survive, and fortunately a shepherd came along a few hours later and found you. I'm sorry, Artie,' he lent down and hugged me again. 'Do you want me to stick around? I'm happy to lose Tahina, I don't really like the girl to be honest, but Pacino will be pissed.'

'No. No, it's fine,' I lied, shaking him off. 'You go, have fun. I'll see you tomorrow?'

'Bright and early. We'll talk then,' he reassured me, then he kissed me on the forehead as he always did. At the door he stopped and turned.

'Hey, Artie?'

'Yeah?'

'I left you a line in the kitchen, in case you couldn't sleep.'

I heard him jog down the stairs to meet his plaything, slamming the door on the ground level and laughing out into the street. I wheeled into the kitchen and stared at the line, which was by no means small. Eventually my nihilism overtook me and I did it, then I went back to the stereo and turned the music up as Concerto 2 began. I resumed position by the balcony and stared out over the sea, trying to understand what my uncle had just told me. Suicide? My father had committed suicide when I was a boy. Suicide was the thing I hated most in the world. I looked at the stars and wondered how it could be true, what single event could have led me to that decision, the last of all decisions. The problem was my memory was blank, so it was destined to remain a mystery. I turned my attention to the sea. By now the beach was silent, the crowds had retired to bed, the lovers had quenched their thirst and the teenagers had abandoned the break-wall. The blanket of melancholy which had kept me warm just an hour earlier was now a toxic rag of depression, torn from end to end, dragged through the mud, trampled over by an unwelcome truth and pissed on by an inescapable past. I pulled out the email from Julia, it said nothing worth noting. What a waste of time she turned out to be.

That night I didn't sleep; Beethoven, Mozart, Chopin, they didn't sleep either. Slowly the dark of night melted into dawn and I wheeled myself into my room. I heard Emilio wake up and rise from the den of the dead fascist. He walked into the kitchen where the remnants of cocaine greeted him.

'Artie! No, no, no!' he cried.

For whatever reason, hearing that made me smile, a cynical, depressed smile, and at last I slept.

6

It's probably the right time in the story to reflect on my injuries a little, although it was almost impossible for me to know if they were healing or not. The pain in my wrists had eased up considerably as the bones went about fusing themselves into new, less mobile forms, while my legs, still heavily cast, were aching less and less each day. I knew I wasn't helping things by drinking so much but I wasn't sure what else to do. The days were long in the apartment, very long, and during poor weather it was no longer possible for me to fill the time watching the parades of people below going about their summers. During good weather I was filled with a pulsating jealousy as I watched those below enjoying their lives. I tried to read but couldn't get into any of the books on the tenor's shelves, I sat down to write but I found I had nothing to say. For all the travelling I'd done over the years, I was an empty well when it came to insights or original thoughts. Emilio would come and go, as he still had duties to fulfil at the hospital from time to time, and the second he'd close the door I'd reach for the bottle. By the time he'd return home I'd make every effort to appear sober and just go to my room and continue drinking. Physically I was healing, at least I seemed to be, but mentally I was deteriorating at a breakneck speed.

In fact, the following weeks played out like a duel with busted pistols, with Emilio and me at odds over everything and agreeing on almost nothing. The cocaine incident didn't go down well but I was able to pass the blame onto Tito's child bride, and then I had to let Tito know Emilio wasn't about to welcome her back, and he reassured me the night had ended poorly enough for that to be a non-issue. Just like every woman my uncle had ever been with, she was tossed out as easily as a carton of two week old milk. For whatever reason it made sense to him to behave like this, but it was a wonder he could still get a date, and I was sure it left him empty.

After waking up from a nap one afternoon I wheeled into the kitchen to get myself a drink, maybe a beer, maybe a wine, I was never sure what I wanted after I'd just woken up. Upon opening the fridge I was slightly sickened to see it was bare, well not bare exactly, the cheese, the tomatoes, the orange juice were there, but the beer and wine weren't. I turned around and the shelf beside the window was bare too, no whiskey, no tequila, no rum. I wheeled back in to the living room, about to make Emilio the second fascist to die in his room, when he appeared in front of me, holding a bottle of local red, half-drunk the night before.

'Before you say anything…' he started.

'You got a death wish Emilio?' I interrupted.

'Ah, ah,' he said, stopping me with his finger, wagging it like a headmaster, 'I want to make a deal.'

'I've got a deal for you, Emilio, re-stock the fridge and we won't be having wheelchair races down the hallway.'

'How are you going to put anyone in a wheelchair, Artie? In your state you'd lose a fight with a kitten. A dead kitten.'

I wheeled towards him and he leapt over the couch, still brandishing the wine. 'Now listen, Arthur. It's bothered me for some time, but I never said anything because you were my patient. But now it's gotten to the point where I have to step in a do something.'

'Emilio, my drinking is not a problem,' I lied, 'it relaxes me, it helps me deal with the boredom of living with you. I'm Australian – we drink!'

'I'm not talking about the drinking, Arthur, you can poison yourself however you like, it's not my business how you die.'

'Well, actually, it kind of is,' I reminded him.

'It's time Artie, that you started to learn Spanish. You're going to be here for a few more months at least so it can only help you.'

'I already speak Spanish.'

Emilio started laughing. He camped it up a notch and started rolling around on the couch in hysterics. It made me second-guess his potential as an actor.

'Alright, fine, I don't speak Spanish, I admit it. But I've tried to learn before and it's too damn difficult.'

'Yes,' he stopped laughing, 'because your mind has been demented by this shit,' he said, indicating the bottle. 'After every hour of study you're allowed one glass.'

'One bottle.'

'Half a bottle.'

'Half a bottle and two beers.'

'Deal.'

'But why Spanish, don't they speak Basque here?'

'They speak both. We can learn Basque too if you like?'

'Baby steps, Emilio,' I said, as he passed the bottle over the couch and I took my medicine.

That's how the daily Spanish classes with Emilio began. It turned out I did know some Spanish but not nearly enough to have a conversation. We'd finish the sessions by reading the newspaper together and translating it. One subject in particular kept popping up with alarming regularity.

'What's the go with these ETA guys?' I asked.

'They want freedom for the Basque country,' he shrugged, as if that were enough to explain it — the bombings, the kidnappings, the everything—explained away with a shrug.

'Excuse the language,' I started, 'but if I look out the window right now it looks pretty fucking free in Basque-land to me, people can do whatever they like here. There's about a half-dozen old blokes on the beach every day with their balls hanging out the sides of their swimming costumes. If that isn't freedom what is?'

'Not that kind of freedom, Arthur, they want more than the freedom to hang their balls out in public, they want their own nation, the right to govern themselves, speak their own language. And actually they have a lot of soldiers in prison who aren't free.'

'Soldiers or terrorists?' I asked, 'Because I'd hardly call a person who blows up civilians a soldier.'

'It's down to perspective, I suppose, although no-one agrees with targeting civilians, myself included. They used to only target the military and the government but somewhere along the way it became toxic.'

'The dead fascist in your room, you think ETA killed him?'

'Sorry? What dead fascist in my room?'

'Oh, nothing, just something my uncle said.'

'We're swapping rooms after dinner.'

'Like hell we are.'

Five bombs had gone off in Cantabrian resort towns, killing no-one and injuring just one. One of the towns was Laredo, where I was heading when I decided to jump off a cliff. Jumped, fell, or pushed? I had no idea. Predictably my uncle hadn't turned up the morning after he told me the news, but he did ring the house to see how I was going. I said I was fine, but I wasn't, really. I refused to believe that's what had happened, and I was eager to do what the doctor suggested and drive out to the place where I fell, to see if any memories came back. The problem was it was on a mountain by the coast, and it'd be a while yet before I could physically manage to go back there. I wheeled over to the window.

'Do you think I'll go mad being cooped up inside here?' I asked Emilio.

He looked up from the newspaper. 'Mad or madder?'

'I'm being serious. It hasn't been that long and I'm already becoming frustrated,' I sipped on my wine. 'If this goddamn building had a lift I could go out every now and then.'

'Where would you go?' he asked.

'Somewhere, anywhere. Probably McDonald's to be honest.'

'McDonald's, that's the place you choose when you're finally free again?'

'Yeah, I'd say so, it's a good McDonald's here. It's comfortable, I like it.'

Emilio shook his head and let out a grunt of exasperation, 'You're in one the food capitals of the world and all you want is McDonald's.'

'You know, I can actually read the chalkboards with this thing,' I said, ignoring him as I scanned the cafes through the telescope. 'All these places are more expensive than McDonald's anyway. It's a purely financial decision, don't take it personally.'

'Stop looking at the chalkboards and start looking at the waitresses,' he demanded. 'I'm becoming worried you're asexual.'

'I can assure you I'm not, before I injured myself I was a regular Casanova in these parts.'

'If you're Casanova then I'm the King of Spain,' he joked, 'and my first order as King — no more balls on the beach!'

'You're a regular fascist,' I replied dryly.

I continued scanning, almost bored enough to find another drink, when one particular waitress caught my eye. And then time stopped, just like that, timelessness, and — apart from my beating heart — perfect stillness.

She wore black sneakers, white socks, black jeans, a black apron and a black t-shirt – midriff. She had tinted skin, a thin, elegant neck supported by two hopelessly fragile shoulders, hair the colour of terracotta tiles on a bombed-out villa, a nautilus spiral on the nape of her neck and eyes like ice and sea and sky. Nature.

'Emilio! Come here!' I shouted, my voice coming alive for the first time since the accident, 'You gotta see this!'

7

'Are you sure it's her?' Emilio asked.

'Yes,' I responded, frustrated by his persistent questions.

'But are you really sure?' he kept on.

'For the last time, yes!'

'And if it's not?'

'Emilio will you please just listen to me, I would recognise that girl anywhere, how could I forget her?'

'I'll tell you how, by jumping,' he said before back-peddling, 'sorry, falling off a cliff and suffering a severe concussion and forgetting everything right up to the point where you magically remember her as perfectly as you remember your own name, not to mention this was someone you met when you were blind drunk, which shouldn't surprise anyone,' he muttered under his breath, driving his point home.

I pushed Emilio away from the telescope and looked again. She carried a tray with five coffees on it, effortlessly, elegantly even.

'When was the last time you felt something for someone, Emilio?' I grilled him.

'I feel contempt for you every day, why?'

'Ah huh, that's just it, that's the thing, everything has to be a joke with you because you can't accept truth, won't accept truth. You don't allow yourself to be anyone other than the perfect Catholic son your mother always wanted. Or the clown.'

'That's shit and you know it,' he rebutted, clearly hurt.

She placed the coffees down and returned to the bar to get some water.

'It's not shit, Emilio. Why are you a nurse? Why were you never an actor?'

'It's not practical to be an actor, I don't want to starve.'

'My uncle is hardly starving. All those actresses he brings home, they might look like they are but I can guarantee that they're not starving either.'

'Your uncle looks like the Greek god Ares, it's different.'

'That old excuse, poor you Emilio.'

She placed the water glasses on the table and filled them, seeing to the women first.

'Why don't you have a girlfriend, Emilio?'

'I don't want a girlfriend.'

She went to another table now, took their order, collected their menus.

'Ok, why don't you have a boyfriend then?'

He was silent a moment. I tore myself away from Coco and looked at him.

'Because.'

'Because why?'

'Because it'd break my mother's heart.'

'Not good enough, things have changed since Franco died, being a gay actor is hardly a subversive act anymore. Look at what Almodovar has done, or would you prefer that he'd locked himself away as well?'

I looked back to Coco, she was gone. My face went tense with panic until she eventually reappeared and looked over the floor, hands on her hips. She shrugged her shoulders and turned around.

'What's your point, Arthur?'

'My point is that you have to believe me when I say it's her, because when I was in that hospital she was the only goddamn thing I could remember when I closed my eyes and tried to understand why my whole goddamned life had been fucked up by some unknown accident that was hidden from me, hidden from me by you and everybody else for your own sick reasons, the one thing that kept me sane was a memory of her blue eyes and a blue boat and when I look out this telescope right now at that quaint little café by the sea, amongst another sea of a thousand pairs of eyes, the only eyes I see are hers. They're like the eyes of an arctic wolf staring out over the tundra, searching for prey, and I'll never forget those wolf-eyes, I'll never be able to forget them, I'll never want to forget them. I could marry a half dozen times and on my deathbed it'll be her eyes I'll tell my grandchildren about. And you'll never understand how a person can claim to not forget eyes because you've never allowed yourself to stare into eyes or to express yourself or to live or to love because you're like all the Spaniards your age, too goddamn scared to move into the twenty-first century. You think you're still a third-world country with a few fancy churches and you think that's enough. But I'm not scared, and she wasn't scared either. And I can guarantee if you went down to her right now and said 'Hi, is your name Coco?' she'd say 'Yes,' and then you'd say 'Do you remember a kid called Arthur, you met him in a bar during a storm?' she'd say 'Yes, I remember Arthur as well as I remember to collect the menus after I take an order,' and then you'd say 'Do you remember a boat, it was blue and white but mostly blue?' and she'd say nothing, she'd just cry. She'd just start balling up like no-one's around and she'd tear off her little black apron and walk across that golden beach and drown herself in the sea. You don't understand why because you don't want to understand why.'

I stopped ranting. Emilio had tears running down his cheeks, I suppose he understood something after all.

'Then I'll go,' he said, solemnly.

'Go where?' I asked, the knot of viciousness still clotting up my throat.

'To the café, I'll walk up to her and I'll say "Hi, is your name Coco?"'

'No you won't.'

'Yes, I will, then I'll say "Do you remember a

kid called Arthur, you met him during a storm?"' he reached for his jacket.

'No.'

'Yes, and then I'll ask, "Do you remember a boat, it was blue and white but mostly blue?"' he put on his hat.

'Emilio, please no,' my hands were shaking now.

'Why no?'

'Not today. Not ever. She can't see me like this,' I looked down at my legs, they disgusted me.

'You're ashamed of your injuries?'

'Wouldn't you be?'

'Not at all. I'd tell her it happened while wrestling a lion.'

'There are no lions in Spain.'

'A tiger then.'

'There are no tigers.'

'Fine, a bear.'

'We wouldn't be able to make love, Emilio.'

'Is that all you care about? That whole speech about wolf-eyes and drowning in the sea and fancy churches and all that other crap was only justification to fuck the girl? A typical fucking poet you are.'

'No! Nothing like that. It's more innocent than that. We met as lovers, Emilio, and if we can't be lovers then maybe it's best we just never meet again.'

I wheeled myself into my bedroom and closed the door. As I did so I heard Emilio take off his hat and jacket. I turned to the mirror and I looked like shit, too thin, too gaunt with tired eyes and a greying beard. I looked old, like a smoker after receiving bad news or a fifty-year-old cocaine addict who never took the time to grow up, never made the effort, never knew he had to. None of the energy was there anymore, just a tired and self-loathing drunk. I took a bottle of whiskey out from the secret stash in the cupboard next to my bed and drank until it was either empty or I passed out. I'll let you decide that one. For the next five days and nights it rained without respite and Coco didn't show for work.

8

San Sebastian was a depressing place for the rain to settle in, which served as a follow-up punch to the depression I could already feel myself sinking into. The ultramarine blue of the Atlantic had been muddied into a cruel and callous grey, the rolling waves now spluttered and foamed like the flush of a urinal. The mountains to the east of the sea had lost their luminous green and became the shadows of beached whales shrouded and buried in fog, their last breath spent long ago. No longer did the fishermen set out each morning in search of marlin, nor did the tours of kayaks explore the cliff faces for secret swimming holes. No longer did the opera house light up blue or green or orange. Lovers didn't wrestle like pups on the sand, teenagers didn't mix drinks by the break-wall, and the cafes didn't bother opening. It'd become a ghost town in the midst of what should be the busiest time of the year, a time of reckless hedonism and ruthless indulgence against the backdrop of sea, sun and sangria. The rain itself was not just vertical but swept across the skies horizontally like a gull in a storm, and I was forced to keep the windows and balcony doors closed tight at all times. Often I'd wheel to the place where the telescope was and check if by chance she'd turned up to work, perhaps to collect a pay packet, perhaps to cover a shift, perhaps because she knew I was watching out for her, some voice on the wind having told her so, a feeling in her gut leading her back to me, but she didn't.

Javier turned up though, and this made my involuntary confinement all the more difficult to endure. Javier was a cousin of mine, Tito's son from an affair which died off twenty-five years ago without so much as a whimper. Tito couldn't stand him and nor could I, and I was pretty sure Emilio was bound to detest him too, despite how good-looking Javier was. But at the end of the day he was Tito's son and he was my cousin and in Spain you tolerate family or you go home. And I couldn't go home, could I? Both my legs were broken.

One afternoon, midway through a Spanish lesson with Emilio, translating an article which sensationalised more ETA attacks, the doorbell buzzed.

'It's Tito, I've brought lunch,' the voice announced through the intercom. Lunch, it turned out, was a home-cooked *paella* which Tito had made that morning. 'I had to hide it walking through the street,' he confided, 'it's a mortal sin to serve *paella* in the Basque country.'

Javier, who occasionally worked in San Sebastian

and otherwise never strayed far from Zarautz where he lived, entered the apartment behind him, ignoring Emilio and me completely. Zarautz was a seaside town about thirty kilometres to the west of here, a place I walked through on the Camino—according to my pilgrim's passport anyhow. Javier enjoyed a laid-back existence there, teaching foreign girls how to surf during the day and how to undress in the evening, all the while putting his feet up in a lavish beachside apartment Tito had purchased for him. Javier's head was shaved, which accentuated his piercing green eyes and high cheek-bones. His body was like that of any avid surfer—chiseled to perfection by the sea and strong like a bull. Yet there was a malice to his beauty that made him frightening, a hatred behind the eyes which he never bothered to conceal. Maybe he didn't know the bitterness which shone through or maybe he did know and wanted everyone to fear it. Either way his presence almost automatically ruined any evening and this one was sure to be no exception. Tito confided in me once, after a few too many drinks, that he was certain Javier would turn out to be a psychopath and he'd spent a fortune putting him up in Zarautz so he wouldn't be around when he finally snapped, he wouldn't have to see the carnage, wouldn't have to clean up the mess. He was also a huge pot smoker and before he'd said a word to anyone he'd already opened the balcony doors and lit up a joint. The rain came sweeping in, drenching everything in reach, and he seemed to enjoy the chaos while the rest of us looked on bewildered.

'Javi,' Tito called across the room, 'you don't remember your cousin?'

'Yeah, I remember you,' Javier said as he walked over to me, reaching out his well-built, heavily tattooed arm to shake my hand. We'd met a couple of times a few years ago and hadn't gotten along so well. 'You still don't speak Spanish then?'

'No, regrettably, but Emilio is teaching me, trying to anyway,' I answered as I turned to Emilio, who shook his head in disapproval, indicating he was already not a fan.

'Arthur has no need for Spanish in Australia, it's normal,' interjected Tito, trying to save me from a grilling.

Javier said something in Spanish which I half understood, something along the lines of 'Shouldn't he speak the native language of the country he is in?' and Tito responded in English, 'Yes but in this house we're going to speak English, Arthur is a guest and when he's ready to speak Spanish then we all can.'

'It's fine Tito, I don't mind what language you speak,' I responded, trying to avoid an argument.

'Oh thank you so much,' Javier mocked, 'the Australian gives us permission to speak our own language in our own country.'

Emilio looked to me and said nothing, then he got up and excused himself. 'I'll prepare the *paella*,' he said, moving in to the kitchen to escape the tension. Tito was fuming but ignored his son and sat with me.

'Have you been well?' he asked.

'Yeah I've been alright.'

'Has the doctor been coming still? What was her name?'

'That was Dr. Rodriguez. It's a different one now, some old guy, nice though. He was here yesterday, and everything seems to be healing as it should. Emilio is taking good care of me, especially when it comes to the simple things like going to the bathroom. The days are long though, especially when it rains. They're getting harder and harder to fill. I've tried reading, writing, everything, and I can't get into any of it. I'm lucky I have the view, though.'

'You know it really upsets me that you can't come and go as you please,' he said, rubbing my shoulder, 'let me ask around and see if there's anything on a ground floor nearby, somewhere you can come and go from, it'll make your life a little more interesting.'

'No it's fine, really, I actually do like it here, I'd miss the view if I left.' The only thing keeping me sane anymore was the chance to catch a glimpse of Coco again. 'Besides, the doctor said it won't be too long now.'

Emilio reappeared from the kitchen with four plates of *paella*, effortlessly carrying two on each arm. If he couldn't make it as an actor then he'd certainly give waitering a decent crack. I wheeled over to the circular table and took a place with Tito on my left, Emilio on my right, and Javier directly opposite. He was staring at me intensely, an unreadable madness flashing through his eyes. I looked away and silently cursed my uncle for having brought him.

'Thank you, Tito,' I said. He smiled in response.

We began to eat while Javier shoved at the seafood in his plate, moving it side to side like a crab shifting sand.

'This is excellent,' commented Emilio, his mouth half full of rice and chicken. 'You know, being a Basque I never got to eat *paella* growing up, my parents refused to cook it. I tried to make it once and failed terribly, it was truly shit! But I still forced everyone to eat it as the ingredients were so expensive; nothing is cheap in the Basque Country anymore. However, as good as it tastes, *paella* is still a sin here,' he said, laughing as he uncorked a bottle of red wine from a local vineyard and poured four glasses until it emptied.

'I can understand that,' said Tito, his mouth half full. 'You have your own food which you're proud of, as you should be, it's some of the best in the world. Unfortunately, though, I can't cook a hell of a lot, and preparing a plate of *pintxos* has always been beyond my talents,' he shrugged. 'To be fair,' he continued, 'I've never had to cook. When I was a young boy in Madrid my mother wouldn't let anyone near the kitchen, not even to flip the sardines or drag the tomato across the bread. If we tried to interfere we'd get a wooden spoon across the back of the head and nothing to eat. Then in my teens I got into film and became an actor and every meal of the day was provided for me. Then as I grew into my years and became a rich man I only ever ate in restaurants, really fucking good restaurants, some of the best in the world, so cooking was a part of life I missed out on. But I did learn how to make a *paella*, off Javi's mother actually, she was from Valencia, where *paella* was born.'

'This is too dry,' Javier interrupted as rice escaped down his chin and dribbled onto his lap.

'Have you been to Valencia?' Tito asked me, ignoring his son. I was about to answer when Javier chimed in again.

'Really, Tito, why is it always too dry? My mother didn't teach you shit.'

'My son is never satisfied,' Tito said, refusing to look in Javier's direction, keeping it together for the sake of Emilio and me.

'I haven't, Tito,' I said, taking my turn to keep things civilised. 'I haven't been to Valencia, but I'd like to go, maybe before I return to Australia when my legs have healed.'

'I'm not saying it's entirely shit,' Javier continued, either unable to read the situation or reading it too well. 'I just said it's too dry. And it is, way too dry.'

'I don't think it's too dry,' offered Emilio, his turn to keep the peace. 'I think it's great, Tito.'

'Did anyone ask you?' Javier challenged him, causing the three of us to fall silent. I put down my fork and glared across the table at him, Emilio was far too easy a target, but Tito butted in before I had the chance to say or do anything.

'The *paella* is too dry,' Tito began mocking his son, 'the apartment is too small, the Spanish are too proud. Next he'll blame me for that bomb going off in Orio yesterday.'

Javier raised his head and stared at Tito like a tiger about to finish off its prey. It was hard to imagine what his mother must have been like for him to be the way he was, as his father was the gentlest, most easy-going man I'd ever met.

'I don't blame you for the bomb, *padre*, but maybe I will blame you for it not having killed anyone.'

'What did you fucking say?' snapped Tito, throwing down his fork and rising to his feet.

'I said…' Javier paused a moment, choosing his words carefully, 'that maybe it's a shame the bomb in Orio didn't kill anyone. How do you say it in English? You have to crack a few eggs to make an omelette.'

Hearing this Tito slapped his son across the face with the entire surface of his giant hand. The room fell silent and no one dared move.

'Don't you ever side with those fucking terrorists again, you understand me? What they do is sick and twisted and I will not have my own son be a cheer-leader for them!'

Javier remained silent a moment longer. I could see he was searching for the best response, the barb that would sting his father the most.

'I suppose it wouldn't be great publicity for the pro-digious film producer to have a terrorist son; perhaps the whores won't drop to their knees so quickly then.'

It worked, Javier got what he wanted. You could see the fire rise up from Tito's gut as he slapped his son again, even harder this time, breaking the skin, and then again and again and again. Javier remained still, his eyes locked shut as he drew a deep breath and blood started to leak from the wound on his cheek. Tito stood frozen as Emilio and I slowly backed away from the table. Javier placed his cutlery neatly beside his bowl, got up from his chair and collected his weed paraphernalia. He walked over towards the door, his eyes downcast the entire time, and opened it.

'You'll have to excuse me, Arthur, and your friend too,' he said. Tito's ferocity had seemingly broken him for the night. 'My father doesn't like discussions, he is far too stubborn for that. He prefers to be the master, shouting out orders like a general in Franco's army, like Franco himself, and I can't be fucked to listen to it tonight.' He walked out of the apartment and slammed the door for effect. Emilio and I let out a sigh and a shared look of dismay, but Tito remained tense and shaken.

'I don't know what I did to deserve that monster,' Tito said as he sat back at the table.

After a few minutes, with the evening slipping away from us, Emilio tried to lighten the mood. 'It's really very good, not dry at all,' he said, having another mouthful of the paella. His attempt had failed. Tito ignored him. Instead he pushed his plate away and pulled out his wallet, reached inside, and pulled out a small half-empty bag of cocaine.

'Is anyone offended?' he asked, flicking his eyes between Emilio and me. I turned to Emilio before shaking my head and he followed suit. It wasn't our business what habits Tito had, but I could tell it was quite confronting for Emilio, who no doubt spent a lot of his career as a nurse tending to addicts and those recovering from addictions. Tito took out his keys, dipped one in and brought the cocaine close to his nose. He snorted it up with the enthusiasm of a pig at its trough. Then he repeated this action twice more.

'Sometimes,' Tito started, his hands becoming animated, 'I want to grab him by the neck and fucking choke him, strangle the little shit until his body goes limp and toss him into the river.' He rose back into his chair and cleared his nasal passage with a roar. 'Fuck!' he yelled, his eyes closed tightly, his jaw clenched, his voice like a wounded bull. He was becoming frightening. 'Ok, I'm sorry, I'll calm down. I'll calm down,' he said, breathing deeply, his eyes still closed. 'Arthur,' he turned to me. 'I'd offer you some coke but it's not healthy, besides I only have a little left.' I assured him that was fine, I really didn't want any and Emilio agreed he didn't need any either. I knew my uncle had a weakness for anything that could make him feel alive and in the moment, anything that could give him that rush he got from being on a red carpet or finally bedding a woman he'd spent years pursuing—but I hadn't realised he was battling a full blown cocaine addiction. I wasn't sure if I should be worried for him or dismiss it as a harmless bit of fun. Either way, I wasn't going to waste my time tonight trying to decide. There were more pressing things on my mind, like trying to remove the dark cloud that had settled in the apartment. I was vulnerable myself, and I needed the place to brighten up a little or I was certain it'd be another sleepless night alone with my thoughts, alone with the bottle, the last thing I needed.

'Who wants to play cards?' I asked. Emilio and Tito both agreed it was a good idea. The night was still young enough to be salvaged and no-one felt like going to bed just yet, especially not Tito now he was pumped full of energy like a *torero* before the *corrida*. Emilio stood up and went over to the tenor's CD collection and put on a Miles Davis album, and found some playing cards on the bookshelf, hidden amongst biographies of giants from the twenty-first century— Einstein, Picasso, Mussolini, Castro. 'Anyone know a game?' he asked. They were Spanish cards, not the standard deck I was used to, and Tito tried to teach us something called '*Chinchon*', the idea being to collect seven cards of the same suit. We tried a few hands, but Tito was too distracted. Not only was he rubbish at explaining the rules, he couldn't stay focused long enough to finish a game. The cocaine was reaching a crescendo inside his mind. His eyes widened again, and he sucked his lips. He was in the mood to talk, not to play games. He put the cards aside and started ranting about his son. The night was well and truly defeated.

'You know, Javi wasn't always like this,' he said as he did another bump of coke off his key, the bag almost empty now. 'He was a good boy when he was younger. Something happened in school though. His mother gave him free range to do whatever he pleased, stay out after school, disappear for entire weekends, which can be dangerous in the Basque Country, dangerous anywhere I suppose, there is always evil lurking in the shadows waiting to pounce on disillusioned, impressionable young men.' He stopped a moment to finish his glass of wine. 'But at the end of the day it's my fault, I should've been there more, I was too busy playing the movie star or the film producer, making more cash for the studios than any other producer, most of them twice my age, working my fucking ass off. You see I never wanted a child, I knew I'd never be there for it, but his mother, despite being as big a whore as I was, was a staunch Catholic and once she was pregnant there was no talking her out of it—God knows I tried—the thing is I didn't want him then, and I don't want him now and the bastard knows it.'

'If it makes you feel better, Tito, there's no way you were worse than my father,' said Emilio, trying to drag him out of the quicksand of self-pity. 'He was a proper son-of-a-bitch who never worked an honest day after he was given an early pension by that filthy fascist Franco for services during the war. He'd spend all day and evening at the bar, keeping company with *Falange* scum just like himself, then he'd come home blind drunk and beat my mother just for a laugh, right in front of me. I wasn't allowed to leave the room, I had to stay and watch, and if I showed the slightest sign of emotion I'd get beaten also. Which of course was every time. It's no wonder I turned out the way I did.'

'And what way are you?' Tito pressed.

'Afraid of everything.'

'You don't seem afraid to me,' Tito said, 'you seem like a man who knows who he is and what he stands for.'

'I'm a closet homosexual, Tito. If that doesn't say afraid what does?'

'Well,' Tito smiled, 'I think with that admission you're officially out of the closet.'

Emilio laughed. 'I suppose I am.'

'Emilio wants to be an actor,' I interrupted, trying to steer the conversation away from having to talk about my own father. Emilio turned to me, appalled. 'I told him you might be able to help him out?'

'Have you done any acting before?' Tito asked.

'Just at school, and in front of the mirror of course.'

'I know everyone there is to know, in Spain at least. Are you interested in the theatre or just the screen?'

'The theatre of course, it's the greatest of all the art forms, so said Oscar Wilde anyhow. And he should know!'

'I have a friend who runs a theatre in Bilbao; it's not a major one, but it's one of my favourites in Spain. I can put you in contact. Maybe you could audition for something?' Tito offered.

Emilio went silent, then he lunged across the table at my uncle and hugged him around the neck tightly, showering his forehead with kisses. Tito pulled back laughing. 'This deserves a toast,' Emilio proposed, picking up an empty wine glass. 'To Tito Ramiro Ramirez, and to Arthur, whose last name I either cannot remember, or I do not know, and to the theatre, which shall be the death of me if she is kind enough to have me!' We all laughed and brought our glasses together.

Emilio sat down enjoying the evening at last, and then brought the attention back to me. 'And you Arthur, you've been hiding over there in the dark, avoiding talking about anything of substance as you so often do. What is your father like?'

Tito and I made eye contact, offering one another

consolation, wondering who would have the guts to speak first. It was Tito.

'Arthur's father was my older brother. He...' Tito stopped and glanced my way.

'He killed himself when I was four,' I said, finishing Tito's sentence. 'I don't remember my father, but I understand he was a good enough man.'

'No, he was a great man,' Tito corrected me.

'I am so sorry,' Emilio started, rising to his feet to hug me. 'Had I any idea I wouldn't have brought it up.'

'It's ok,' I said, gently pushing his huge weight off me, 'I guess it's important he is remembered sometimes, brought up at tables just like this. There's been entire years when I haven't even thought about him, not once, not for a second. Although recently he's been on my mind a lot, for obvious reasons.'

'I'm always here to talk,' Emilio assured me. I shook my head, implying it wouldn't be necessary. 'God, I feel so stupid,' he lamented as he sat back down.

I never asked my mother any questions about my father, as what I knew about him already was shocking enough. He'd come to Australia on his own at twenty-four, on a ship from the Galician port city of Vigo, supposedly fleeing gambling debts here in San Sebastian. He had no English skills and was only able to secure work as a cleaner for a newspaper in an inner-city suburb, which was typical work for migrants entering Australia back then, despite the fact he'd been an engineer in Spain. While working at the newspaper he met my mother, who was a secretary. She gave him late night English lessons to earn some cash on the side and eventually they fell in love, although his English never really improved while she became fluent in Spanish. Nine months later I was born, which added a financial strain that my parents couldn't manage. The marriage deteriorated to the point where they could barely smile anymore let alone love one another. My father was heavily depressed, not satisfied with bringing home the measly wage of a cleaner, and started drinking as a way to disguise his shame and protect his pride. It was in the shady bars on the outskirts of inner-city Sydney that he got mixed up in crime and, like in his youth, gambled, until he'd run afoul of the wrong person and had accumulated debts he'd never be able to pay. So he hung himself in the top floor bathroom of a Surry Hills hotel, something he probably figured was a just punishment for himself, although he must have known he was leaving my mother and me for dead. My uncle insisted my father was a great man but nothing in his biography made me think so, at least nothing I was ever told, and I figured it was best to resign his memory to the past. His ghost was only ever present when I was either very drunk or very lonely, which right now was basically every day. Besides, his suicide eventually sent my mother mad and I could never forgive him for that. She never spoke Spanish again after he hung himself and she saw to it that I was never taught.

'Can we change the subject?' I asked.

'Good idea,' Tito nodded. 'Let's talk about women, let's talk about Julia, Arthur, are you going to convince her to come to Spain and reignite the flame?'

'No,' I replied flatly. 'In her last email she barely said a word. I have no feelings for her anymore and it's obvious she has no feelings for me. It was as clean a breakup as you could possibly hope for.'

'Ah, don't be so sure, the reason I bring it up is she emailed you again the other day. We need to set you up with a computer here or I'll start charging you a secretary's fee.'

'What did she say?'

'I didn't read it, I had one foot out the door already, but I read the title, it simply said 'I miss you.''

Emilio cleared his throat and Tito and I turned our attention to him. He had that smug look on his face he got when he was hiding something from someone. I cringed at what it might be.

'What?' I asked.

'Blue eyes … a blue boat …' Emilio teased. I warned him to stay quiet.

'I'm confused, is there something you're not telling me?' Tito asked.

'Nothing,' I responded, sharply, flatly, attempting to end the discussion.

'Bullshit,' Emilio laughed.

'What is it?' probed Tito.

'Our young cripple here is in love, what else?'

'With whom?' Tito pressed.

'With blue eyes and a blue boat,' Emilio burst out laughing. I reached over to slap him across the head, but he pulled out of reach of my swing, causing me to plunge across the table as his laugh grew.

'It's nothing, Tito, our friend over here just doesn't

know when to keep his fat mouth shut,' I said. Tito did another bump of cocaine, the last in the bag.

'It clearly doesn't sound like nothing,' he said.

Emilio jumped up out of his chair and moved behind the couch, a spot he knew I couldn't access in my chair.

'A week ago, your darling nephew sat at the telescope and started panning the tight asses of all the waitresses on the esplanade.'

'Good boy,' Tito said.

'That's not what happened!' I interjected. Tito stood up and covered my mouth with his massive hands.

'Continue,' he ordered Emilio.

'Well, our darling Arthur, having not been able to please himself ever since his unfortunate fall from a cliff, and not allowing me to give a helping hand, thought to arouse his imagination by seeking out the finest San Sebastian had to offer, and we both know, Tito, when it comes to the fairer sex San Sebastian can offer a lot.'

Tito nodded; he knew better than anyone. 'Well, low and behold, Arthur had been hiding from all of us, all this while, the great romance of his young and complicated and quite frankly unfortunate life, a blonde of northern European descent with golden hair and eyes like a fox.'

'Wolf!' I protested through Tito's hand. 'Eyes like a wolf!'

'I took the telescope off him at this point,' Emilio went on, 'to see what the fuss was all about, and I tell you, I could have stripped off my Real Madrid jersey and worn the colours of Barcelona, she was such a beauty. I straight away offered to arrange a sequel for our estranged international lovers. Perhaps you could produce it Tito, although this time it would have to play out in a wheelchair and not the fanciful blue boat so ingrained in his imagination. But alas, in true Arthur fashion, he flatly refused me and sulked off into his room to drink alone, blaming his impotence on his injuries rather than the fact he is entirely without anything even remotely resembling a spine.' He poured himself some more wine, the last thing he needed. 'But as I told him, if she were as hungry a fox as he made her out to be, these plaster casts would be no obstacle for her ravenous mouth!' he burst out laughing and Tito followed suit.

Tito approached me and bent down to my level, his hands now caressing my cheeks rather than suffocating them.

'Young nephew, why did you not tell me you were so sick with love? For a while there I thought perhaps my favourite relation was as dour as all my others.'

'I didn't say anything because I was sure I'd lost her. I was sure I'd never see her again.'

'Where did you first meet her?' he asked.

'In a bar in the old town, I can't remember the name, it's not important I suppose, what is important is she's the last memory I have. I was with her, and then I was in the hospital, gazing up at you.'

'The plot thickens,' Tito gasped. 'I wonder if she tried to murder you?' he laughed.

'Then I saw her last week, not as crudely as Emilio likes to think, when I was panning the esplanade with the telescope, looking at chalkboards and not asses. But I can't see her again. I look and feel pathetic. And even if I wanted to it's impossible, she hasn't shown for work all week.'

'Of course she hasn't,' chimed Emilio. 'The esplanade has flooded all week and Noah is about to ride down in his ark! Do you expect the poor girl to drown for your satisfaction? But the good news is the rain is said to stop tomorrow, so I suppose there's a chance she'll be back at work.'

'I might just have to pay her a visit,' said Tito. 'Which café is it?'

I protested, even begged him not to, made him promise he wouldn't dare. But inside I knew it was the one thing in the world I wanted. The one thing I needed. The one thing that just might save me from my spiral into hell. It wasn't making love to her I craved, it was just seeing her, touching her, knowing her. No doubt my accident and the fact she was my last memory had made her more significant than she might have been otherwise, but that night with her, as drunk as we were, was the most vivid night of my life. Externally I pleaded with Tito not to visit her—a defence I'd prepared in case she rejected me—but internally I was begging him to do just that, for if there was one thing I knew to be true in this world it was that women, of all ages, men too, had a hell of a time resisting my uncle's charms. I didn't want his money, I didn't want his cocaine, I didn't want a fancy apartment by the sea or a shot at being a star. I wanted Coco, and I knew he could deliver.

'Please, Tito, no,' I feigned, 'promise me you won't visit her?'

He just smiled. It was the smile of a God. 'Eyes like a wolf, eh?'

9

'What happened?' she asked, pulling back a stray curl that had collapsed across her forehead.

'I fell,' I answered, feigning a smile to hide the sad, pathetic truth.

'What did you fall off?' she continued, tilting her head to the right.

'A cliff,' I replied, breaking eye contact, surveying the cornices, patterned with vine leaves and a flower every now and then, looking at anything other than her, checking out the carpet—cream-coloured.

'Excuse me?' she laughed, covering her mouth, her eyes lighting up (searchlights at sea.)

'A cliff,' I repeated, returning my focus back to her. She really was beautiful.

'How did you manage to fall off a cliff?' she continued, leaning in to me, close enough to taste her skin.

'I don't know, I have no memory of it happening,' I admitted, flicking my eyes away, then back to her and then away again.

'How do you know you fell then? Maybe you jumped,' she teased, not realising how her comment stung me, not knowing she twisted a dagger inside my chest.

'That's the thing,' I revealed at last, 'I don't know. Maybe I did jump,' I dropped my eyes to hide, to disappear, to vanish. 'No-one knows, no-one will ever know.'

'Oh,' Coco said, leaning back and covering her mouth. Nothing more, just 'Oh.'

The day after Tito had learned of Coco he went and had lunch at her cafe. When he returned he described her as dazzling and her service as impeccable and in his own offensively machismo way he couldn't stop expressing how proud he was of me for having slept with her. He said he'd picked her accent straight away although he'd promised her he wouldn't tell me. He said that for a person who had travelled there was a hell of a lot I didn't know about the world. While Tito had been dining and getting to know Coco, Emilio organised an ambulance and took me to the hospital to have some new x-rays done and hopefully have the cast on my left leg removed. Dr. Rodriguez was there, and she approved; she considered that the left leg had healed well enough to be cut free. When they removed the cast, I was shocked by how thin my leg was. All the muscle had eaten away at itself, and thick black hairs covered it like worms. Emilio shaved

the hairs away, under the pretence that if Coco were
to see them, she'd likely be turned off.

'I wouldn't go near you,' he said as he wet the razor.

When we left the hospital, we drove out to Zarautz
along the Camino path wherever possible, wherever
it followed a road. I didn't recognise anything specific
in Zarautz, but I did get an overwhelming feeling that
I'd been there before. I had a memory of the space if
not the place. We sat by the beach and tried to pick
Javier out from the surfers in the sea, but we couldn't;
they were all more or less identical. We continued discussing Javier over a few beers and it turned out my
estimation was correct; Emilio detested the guy. By the
time we arrived home Tito had organised dinner for
us, just some take-out he got from a local diner. Then
he surprised me with the news that Coco was planning
to come and see me after she had finished work. My
heart began racing like mad. I went in to my room and
looked in the mirror—I looked like shit. I was certain
she'd take one glance at me, worn and weathered and
still in a wheelchair, and she'd regret the day we ever
met.

'Well isn't this convenient, just this morning my
mother went into a rage that I hadn't been home since
I moved out here and I promised I'd spend the night
at hers,' Emilio said.

'I guess you and Coco will have the house to your-
selves then,' Tito said turning to me. 'Will she be able
to look after you though?'

'He may have a hard time showering himself,'
Emilio joked. 'Coco may just have to give him a hand.'

'How will he shit?' Tito asked.

They burst out laughing while I stared at them with faux contempt. To be honest I wasn't really listening to anything that was coming out of their mouths. All I could focus on was the pounding in my chest. My heart was about to explode.

Later that evening, Coco and I sat alone in the living room, not knowing what to say next, the truth seemingly too difficult to indulge in any longer.

'Does it hurt?' she asked.

'Yes, it hurts a lot, but it's getting better, every day is a little easier.'

'So it's ok now?'

'It's better, but not ok.'

'Was it a big cliff?'

'Apparently. Luckily I landed on a ledge, otherwise I was straight into the Atlantic. A shepherd found me, he assumed that I was dead as the eagles had already surrounded me. They were picking at my fingers as if they were little worms. Look,' I said, showing her the scars on my hand, 'I'm lucky they didn't fly off with any.'

'Oh my god,' she said, holding back her laughter, 'you're lucky you're not dead, and you're lucky you have such a cool story.'

'It would be cooler if I could remember it.'

'That's true. So this is where you live then? It's really beautiful. Is it your uncle's apartment?'

'No, it belongs to a friend of his, a famous opera singer.'

'Sounds fancy. He's a really nice guy, your uncle that is.'

'Yeah, really nice, he's looked after me well.'

'You're lucky to have family here.'

'I suppose I am. What about you? What are you still doing here? I thought you would've gone home by now.'

'You don't remember?'

'No.'

'I told you the next morning, as you left my room.'

'I don't remember much to be honest, although I remember our night together, everything.'

'I don't.'

'You don't?'

'No, I was too drunk. I'm sorry.'

When she said this my heart sank a little. I found it hard to believe that a night which meant everything to me was so easily forgotten by her. If she couldn't remember it no doubt I'd end up questioning the details myself. What if it didn't happen the way I thought it did, what if it were just a dream?

'Do you remember the boat? Please tell me you remember the boat.'

'Not really, maybe some of it. But I can remember the next morning well enough, you were planning to start that walk thing. You were stressed because you couldn't find your keys or something stupid like that. It was raining again, and I asked you to come back to bed and we made love again. Then you rushed off and said you'd find me when you got back. Then I never heard from you and gave up. You don't remember this?'

'Not at all.'

'That's sad, isn't it? We've made love twice now but

each of us only remembers the once. I'm not sure if it's sad or stupid.'

'That's life, I guess, everything in life is either sad or stupid. Or both.'

'True, you're definitely both,' she laughed.

'Thanks,' I said, smiling back at her. 'So what did you tell me? That next morning.'

'That I'm living here, teaching English to Basque children and doing shifts in a café until I work out what I want to do next.'

'And have you worked it out yet, what you want to do?'

'No. I don't know if I ever will, but the café is nice, I like it there, although I'm not sure it's safe with creepy guys watching me through telescopes,' she teased.

'You're too intelligent to work in a café forever.'

'How do you know this? You know nothing about me.'

'The way you speak, the way you know when to laugh or when not to laugh, it tells me you're intelligent.'

'Thank you. You must know, though, that I think you're stupid. Really, really stupid.'

'You do?'

'Of course. Think about it, you don't know if you fell or jumped off a cliff, and then eagles almost ate your hands. That is so stupid. And you don't remember making love to me, which is the stupidest of all.'

'You're right, I am stupid. I should never have left you that morning, I should have stayed and none of this would have happened.'

'I told you to leave, I was excited for your adventure,' she smiled as we sat in the silence for a few moments. 'Can you guess what country I'm from yet?' she asked. 'Or are you too stupid for that too?'

'Ok, I'll try, so long as I can have three chances?'

'Deal, my Australian.'

I brought up a map in Europe in my mind and listed off the first three countries which appeared to me.

'The Netherlands.'

'No.'

'Sweden?'

'Nah-uh.'

'Denmark?'

'Oh my god, you really are stupid. Now you'll never know,' she said, standing up and moving towards the kitchen. 'Do you have wine?' she called out over her shoulder.

'Yes somewhere in the kitchen, hold on I'll get it.'

'No, allow me, I feel like you will fall out the window or something and break even more bones,' she laughed. 'Or jump.'

Coco went into the kitchen as I adjusted myself on the couch. The evening was going well enough I thought, the conversation was easy like I remember it was, and she seemed to be happy to flirt with one another. I was still disturbed however that she had no memory of our night, just the morning after. It made me feel like I'd taken something from her, like I'd hurt her somehow, abused her. When she returned, she had two glasses of red wine, which she placed on the table in front of me. She scanned the room for a moment before moving over to the light switch, dimming the lights to a soft and haunting orange glow. She walked over to the tenor's CD collection and flicked through the titles before selecting one she liked, Nancy Sinatra. She put the music on and turned back to me. I went to say something, but she put a single finger over her lips to suggest I be quiet, she'd be the master tonight. Her arms crossed in front of her as she grabbed the lower hem of her t-shirt and lifted it over her head, revealing a lacy black bra. She undid the bra slowly, letting it fall to the floor before flicking it away with her foot. She moved over to me on the couch and delicately straddled me, all the while being careful not to hurt me, then she put her right breast in my mouth and then her left while my hands crept around to grab her from behind. She began to grind herself into my chest. We were like this for several minutes until the discomfort became too much and sharp pains shot through me. I gently pushed her away, she resisted.

'I'm sorry, Coco, but it hurts.'

'Maybe I can help?' she said as her hands moved towards my groin.

'No, you can't, I'm really sorry but you can't, everything down there hurts. It's pointless trying.'

'It's ok, don't say sorry.'

I looked away, ashamed, as she moved over to the edge of the coffee table, her body language betraying her rejection. We both reached for our wines and took a sip, not making eye contact, not knowing one another, not realising something had to be done, something had to be said. We'd sworn to love each other, not with words but with other things, with gestures and touches, intimate touches, and there we were so close and yet so broken. We were two lost souls in a generation of lost souls, trying to find meaning in one another as meaning existed in nothing else.

'Look,' I said.

'What is it?' she turned to me, shy now, I'd never seen her shy before.

'Take off your pants.'

'But you said…?'

'Don't worry about me, just take off your pants.'

Coco stood up and unbuttoned her jeans, she slid them off like they were never there at all. Then she removed her underwear. There she stood, in the faded orange glow of the baroque apartment with the too high ceilings and cream coloured carpets, with cornices of vines and flowers and the wind from the balcony carrying the scent of the cold and cruel Atlantic into our private palace. Nancy continued to serenade us. I adjusted myself so I was lying flat on the couch. I could see the stars from here. I tried to make out a nautilus spiral in their apparent randomness of form, and then I looked at Coco, timid and raw in her nudity.

'Sit here,' I said, parting my lips.

She moved close to me, she obeyed.

Paradise.

10

During those weeks I didn't just find paradise in Coco, although she was a well that never ran dry, paradise was everywhere in San Sebastian. In those middle weeks of summer the rain had finally exhausted itself and every day was more a gift than the last. The jazz festival had come and gone, with Tito being a guest of honour most evenings while I sat on the balcony and listened to the music whenever the breeze was kind enough to carry it up to me. Otherwise I'd watch friends, families, and lovers intermingle on the esplanade or by the sea, they dressed in their finest for their evening *paseo*—the Spanish tradition of walking around a plaza and catching up with friends in the afternoon hours—and then settled in for drinks, enjoying what would surely be their finest evenings of the entire year, before returning to a life elsewhere of work and stress and sobriety and not of jazz or sea or San Sebastian.

Coco and I settled into a rhythm that was comfortable and true. I was petrified that at some point it might end, petrified of any look in her eyes I couldn't understand. For the first time in years my life developed something akin to meaning, and all thanks to my bond with Coco; in a way I began to worship her even though I knew the risks. I looked at my right leg and willed it to never heal, for me to never leave the apartment, for the tenor to never return, for him to become so famous that San Sebastian would be too small or for his plane to crash in to the Alps on the way to Vienna or for him to be revealed as a spy and banished to a Russian gulag. Anything that would keep him from returning and tearing down my private paradise was good with me. We had a rhythm now, a life together, a little glimpse into our future should we somehow make this work. Coco would finish work around six and come to the apartment, we'd laugh with Emilio and start on the first wines of the day, Tito would swing by, Javier hadn't been seen. We'd prepare a dinner together over a few more drinks, Emilio would retire to bed, Tito would wish us goodnight as he eloped to a meet a lover, and we'd curl up as best we could. We still didn't make love, not in the conventional sense. I was still too wounded for love.

One afternoon Coco suggested we leave the apartment and have a drink together in the old town. At first I thought she was joking, it was true that I spent most of my time free from the wheelchair with a crutch under my arm, but it hadn't occurred to me that this opened up the possibility of a certain kind of freedom. After a brief discussion over the logistics I finally agreed to give it a shot.

Coco supported me down the four flights of stairs, which took no less than twenty minutes, with me having to stop after each step to build the courage for the next. She laughed the entire way; nothing gave her so much satisfaction as laughing at me. As we came out onto the street the sun streaked across my face for the first time in weeks and I was frozen in time, I felt alive again, human almost, reborn certainly. Although my leg hurt like hell.

'The day is warm but the breeze is cold,' Coco said, folding her arms around herself, 'the Atlantic is my least favourite of all the oceans, it makes the air cold even in the height of summer.'

'I've never heard of someone having a least favourite ocean before,' I responded.

'Do you think it makes me weird?' she asked.

'I think it makes you you, it makes you Coco, and Coco is weird.'

She smiled and kissed me, then with one crutch under my arm and one under hers—she begged for a crutch to share in the humility with me—we limped across the plaza through the crowds of excited tourists and dreary locals and into the old town. We stopped at the nearest bar and Coco ordered a carafe of white wine. She arranged some *pintxos* as I waited at a table outside and we watched a busker perform in the square. He was an old man in a Basque beret playing communist anthems on an acoustic guitar. His clothes were tattered, and his voice was ripped and torn, sometimes Spanish and sometimes English, and you could see that the songs meant something to him. From where I was, thirty yards away, I could make out tears in his eyes.

She leaned in to me, entangling her arm in mine, 'I'm happy like this,' she said, softly as if it were a secret, as if the words themselves were dangerous.

'I'm happy too, Coco, the happiest I can remember.'

She looked at me, her eyes glistening like the tide at sunrise, and then she kissed me. 'When do you think it will end?' she asked, pulling away and reaching for her wine.

'What will end? The music?' I responded, taking a sip of wine too.

'No, this,' she said, 'us.'

'Why does it have to end?'

'Everything ends, Artie, don't be such a boy. My life before you ended, and your life before me ended, so this life too will end and then we'll start new lives, which will surely also end. Eventually we'll have run out of lives to end and it will just be the one final end, the biggest end of all. No more new lives and no more new ends, just one final end.'

'When did you start drinking today?' I teased.

'I'm being serious, Artie. I wasn't happy before, but I'm happy now, but it won't last, and I'm trying to get ready for that.'

'Don't talk like this, please, just enjoy the man with the guitar.'

She turned her attention to the musician, collapsing

deeper into my embrace. 'What is he singing about?' she whispered.

'A valley where there was a battle, here in Spain.'

'Who won?'

'Well, the good guys won the battle, but they lost the war.'

'That's always the way, isn't it? The good guys always lose in the end.'

'No, Coco, it's not. I'm a good guy aren't I?'

'No, you're a stupid guy.'

'Ok, but a good stupid guy?'

'Yes, I suppose. More good than bad at least.'

'Well I won the war, didn't I?'

She laughed. 'You think you've won me already? You don't even know me yet Artie, this is what I mean, it has to end.'

'I really wish you'd just shut up today,' I said, pushing her away from me.

She smiled and leant in to kiss me. There was nothing she enjoyed more than riling me up, it was her way of saying I love you.

'Let's go to the sea, I want to see if our boat is still there,' I said.

'Describe the boat to me, I wish I could remember it.'

'It was a regular fishing boat; it was blue and white but mostly blue.'

'Like my eyes?'

'Exactly the same. Except it was a boat, so not the same at all.'

It took a good forty-five minutes to limp to the sea,

to the steel pier with the steps where we'd first touched each other's naked flesh. Where I first saw her shiver like a child and she first reached out for my embrace. The boat was still there, exactly where I remember it, completely unremarkable except for the fact that it existed the night that Coco and I had met.

'Which one is it?' she asked. I pointed it out. 'That's very far, Artie, I could've drowned. Or was that your plan?'

'I was with you the whole time. I can't believe you don't remember it.'

'I remember everything, Artie, I just wanted you to believe I didn't.'

'Everything?'

'Yes, everything, maybe even more than you.'

'Why did you lie then?'

'So it would be easier for you to let me go.'

I pulled her in tighter. 'Good luck getting out of this,' and we kissed.

'I want to swim,' she said.

'I can't,' I replied, shifting my leg.

'I know you can't, but I can.'

She stripped down to her underwear, not caring for the young families or older couples soaking up the sun beside us, and swam out to the boat. I stayed leaning against the railing and watched her, never taking my eyes off her. When she reached the boat she pulled herself aboard with ease, her thin, wiry muscles glistening under the midday sun, and she started simulating sexual acts while laughing hysterically and waving to me. I looked around and the old men to my right pretended not to notice, although one of them lowered his glasses and gave me a wink as his friend elbowed him in the ribs. Coco swam back to me, wet and salty and so damn small, and I wrapped my arms around her, sharing in her wetness.

'It was more fun without you,' she said.

We left the pier and went through the old town back towards the apartment, stopping at no less than four bars on the way. Back in the apartment we went to bed and tried to make love again and still I couldn't. She said she didn't care but she did, of course she did. This is what she meant by the end; it was cruel for things to continue this way. Coco was a realist and I was a dreamer, and that night we both dreamt of the passion of our first meeting, which, despite our deepest desires could never be recreated. Coco would be forever alone on the blue and white boat, having to simulate sex while waving to me stuck on shore. The next morning the realist woke up knowing the end was coming, while the dreamer woke up and made her some coffee.

11

'Two things, Artie,' Tito said, spreading out on the couch as we eased one another through our crippling hangovers, which was too often the case on weekdays. While Coco and Emilio struggled away at work, Tito and I had endless hours to whittle away. Idly wasting away in the living room we'd spend the day discussing everything and nothing at the same time, occasionally interrupting the trickle of conversation with a nap or another drink. Usually another drink.

'Yeah, what's up?'

'Neither of them is good.'

'Ok, what is it?'

'Well, firstly, I'm being awarded a lifetime achievement award at the San Sebastian Film Festival this year.'

'Congratulations, that's fantastic. Isn't it?'

'No it isn't.'

'No?'

'No, Artie, it's shit.'

'How could it possibly be shit?'

'Because… well… because…', he fiddled at the buttons on his red wine stained shirt, undoing them and then doing them back up again, some kind of nervous tick he had.

'Because…?'

'Because I can't get up and talk in front of crowds and cameras without getting completely high off my tits beforehand and making a god damn ass of myself.'

'Tito, you're an actor for fuck's sake. Just act.'

'*Was* an actor, Artie. Emphasis on *was*. And not all actors are show-ponies just so you know, some are shy, humble people who have a need to create, to express themselves, not to shill themselves out for awards or cash or women and wine.'

'You're honestly trying to tell me you're a tortured artist?'

'You're not buying it?'

'No,' I said flatly as I struggled to my feet, 'not in the slightest.' I made my way into the kitchen and grabbed two beers out of the fridge and poured two shots of whiskey. I looked out the window and watched as the early afternoon surfers waited for the swell to pick up. The sky was as blue as I'd seen it all summer. The previous evening Coco and I had gotten drunk after she finished work and she insisted we tried making love again. I gave it my best shot and we almost got there, but again, the pain in my hips and my legs took all the pleasure out of the rest of me. It was becoming clear it was going to be physically impossible, at least for a while and maybe forever. I told her we should probably just stop trying, and in a drunken moment she decided she was the problem and she got dressed and left. She told me not to call her anymore. I tried contacting her all morning, but she was either serious this time or too damn hungover to get out of bed and call me back. Either way, the morning had been a drag, but I did find Tito entertaining right now—the millionaire prince who was too loved and too adored to handle it without the hard and free drugs. What a mess he was, but I loved him for it. I returned to the living room and handed him a shot.

'Arthur it's a bit early for this?'

'I'm not taking life advice off you, Uncle, now drink.' We did the shot. 'So, let's get this clear,' I continued, 'you feel as if you can't function without the coke?'

'That's not what I'm saying.'

'Sure sounds like it.'

'You're missing the point, Artie, the drugs aren't the problem, the drugs are just there to keep me company, like an old friend … ' he stopped himself there. 'That sounds messed up, doesn't it?'

'Very.'

'You didn't do drugs back home?'

'No, I told you, it wasn't a thing.'

'What did you do instead? Apart from drink, obviously,' he said, taking a sip of beer and staring at the ceiling. 'You know,' he continued, 'we never talk about you Artie, you're a complete mystery to me. '

'You're changing the subject.'

He took a drink and shrugged.

'So if the drugs aren't the problem,' I swigged some beer, 'what is then?'

'It's the situation I've gotten myself in, the expectation people have of me. I've never told anyone this before but I'm a total fraud, Artie. I've risen to the top of this industry without ever having done one piece of interesting work, without ever having broken a sweat. I didn't exactly screw my way to the top Artie, but I might as well have; it's not hard to do; god knows some careers have been made by climbing in to bed with me.'

'So you feel like an imposter?'

'Yes! That's the word, imposter.'

'And now you're being given a lifetime achievement award that you feel you haven't earned.'

'Correct!'

'And the speech is scaring the shit out of you because you don't know what to say.'

'Sort of.'

'Sort of?'

'You see here's the thing, I don't want to get up there and dribble some nonsense and have everyone realise I'm a fraud, that the entire persona is a myth and thus costing me my reputation.'

'The reputation you know yourself you don't deserve.'

'Now you're understanding. Reputation is everything here, Artie, you think I can fill my parties with A-listers without it?'

'Probably not. But is this festival really that big a deal? Who's even going to be there?'

'To put it into context, Artie, Meryl Streep is presenting my award.'

'Oh.'

'Oh, indeed.'

'You're going to need some drugs then.'

'Exactly, lots of drugs.'

'And a speech writer.'

'And even more drugs.'

'Let's just start with *some*.'

'And you.'

'And me?'

'Yes Artie, and you. I'm going to need a face in the audience, someone in the front row to make eye contact with if it all gets too much, a friendly face, one I trust.'

'What about your son?'

'Who? Javi? Yeah he'll be there, he always is, but I don't want to make eye contact with him, Artie, he scares the shit out of me. When he was a kid he used to catch frogs in the well and skin them, you ever seen someone skin a frog? They hop around all pink and skinless until they eventually bleed out. I didn't even know it was a thing until I saw my own son do it, he was four years old. I wouldn't be surprised if he skins babies now. No, you, Artie, you'll be my guest of honour, but we'll have to work the red carpet first, so they know we're not gay, that'd make for an interesting morning paper.'

'When is it?'

He reached into his satchel and pulled out a pile of papers. One was the invitation. He put on his glasses and held it at arm's length, trying to read the small font. 'Let's have a look, 18-27 September 2008. I'll be up on opening night, so the 18th. You don't have any plans, do you?' he joked.

'Maybe. For all you know I could be back home in Australia by then.'

'Arthur, don't be an idiot, we both know your home is here with me and Coco and Emilio. You have nothing else. Australia is dead for you.'

I was becoming closer to Tito every day and despite his flaws I liked him anyway. In fact I think it was his flaws that made me admire him, it made him real. Here he was admitting to me he was a drug addict, a fraud, a calculating womaniser with a paper-thin ego and a daddy-didn't-love-me fear of emotional relationships with other men. He had a son he hated, a guest-list who only turned up for the drugs, no talent, no ambition and no one else to talk to apart from me, a distant nephew he barely knew a month ago. And yet he admitted all of this freely, which is what I liked. We're all flawed, god knows I'm as flawed as anyone I've ever met, yet I wasn't about to tell anyone about it, well except for you, reader. When he put his arm around me he felt like a father, someone who cared, albeit a father who now pulled away from me and cut up two lines of cocaine.

'You're having one, kid,' he said.

I did the line, and it felt good, and we sat there and finished the beers and had another and joked about how he might get Meryl Streep into bed. Then he reached into his bag again and pulled out some loose pieces of paper.

'This is the other piece of news,' he said, handing them to me. 'This one's a real shit I'm sorry to tell you.'

They were emails, three of them, all from Julia. Julia hadn't meant anything to me in months, in fact since the return of Coco in my life I hadn't even thought of her once. I was even beginning to forget what she looked like. I knew her hair was brown, but I couldn't tell you the colour of her eyes. The first email was short, it went like this:

Miss you…

Hey Arthur, you didn't reply to my last email, which is fair enough, I guess I didn't give you much to reply to, haha. Anyway I'm really worried about you and hope you're doing well. Can you give me an update on how it's all going? Everyone here misses you, come home soon. Xx

'Come home soon?' What the hell did she mean 'come home soon,'? I didn't have a goddamned home thanks to her kicking me out. This made me angry, I wished I hadn't read it. The next email went:

Exciting News…

Hey Arthur, thanks for not replying again! All good though, you're probably in hospital so I'm not angry. I

I had a heavy feeling in my gut after reading this. While she was keen to profess she wasn't stalking me I'd be hard pressed to call it anything else. What I didn't understand was why? She left me because I wasn't going anywhere in life, and now more than ever before I was literally going nowhere, and fast. If I wasn't enough beforehand I was hardly going to inspire her by sitting in this apartment all day doing drugs with my uncle while spying on Coco at work. This had disaster written all over it, so I did another line. The final email pulled the rug out from under my comfortable little life here.

I turned to Tito, 'Tito, this is very bad news.'

'Yeah, I figured you wouldn't be too excited,' he replied.

'I'm the opposite of excited, I'm going to have an anxiety attack.'

'Best not to do it while the drugs are kicking in, Artie, wait till you're coming down tomorrow. I've got to run,' he said, looking at his watch. 'I'll leave you another line.'

Tito left for a date with an actress who he'd met through his publicist in Madrid while I stayed home and waited for Coco to call. She never did. That night I drank solidly and fell asleep late around 3 a.m. I woke up a couple of hours later needing to use the bathroom but something wasn't quite right with my leg and I couldn't move enough to leverage myself off the edge of the bed. I rang the bell for Emilio but then I remembered he'd arranged to stay at his mother's house again, thinking Coco would be with me. I had no choice but to lay there and piss myself and that's how Emilio found me the following morning, in bed and unable to move, soaked in my own urine. Needless to say I didn't feel great about it, and I wondered what Julia would think if she found me like this. I wondered if she'd still be so keen on stalking me. I wondered if this was the 'direction' she was always on about. I wouldn't say it was the high point of my life, but I wouldn't go so far as to call it the lowest, either.

12

Tito had a friend named Cecilia who he'd met at a party in Cannes fifteen or so years earlier. She used to be a session sailor who'd crew on proper sailing boats for months on end without ever asking for a wage, but without having to pay for food, board or adventure in return—all was included. Eventually she fell in love and married the owner of a sailboat named Ulysses, and when the owner passed away Ulysses was left to her in his will, much to the chagrin of his children, who got very little. It was over 30 feet long with two sails and three cabins and she'd lived on it ever since, sometimes with minimal crew and sometimes completely alone. Tito had organised a day out for all of us on the boat, and while he and Cecilia were enjoying some wine by the port and waiting for us, Emilio fussed around the apartment filling a bag with things we were never going to need.

'Don't forget to pack this,' he said, throwing me a ukulele he found on the shelf.

'Emilio, what the hell do we want this for?' I asked.

'I don't know, maybe someone can play it during the sunset. I'm sure Tito is musical.'

I threw the ukulele back onto the couch.

'Did you find any snorkels?' I asked.

'Snorkels? What do we want snorkels for?'

'For snorkeling.'

'No chance you're getting me in that water. You're Australian aren't you, don't you know the sea is full of sharks?' he asked.

'Fucking hell,' I mumbled to myself.

The morning went on much the same until Coco arrived and we were ready to go and meet Tito and Cecilia. Coco and I had made peace after the split earlier in the week, and we both decided it'd be worth dealing with the frustration rather than just cutting things off. I assured her my impotence was temporary, although the doctor was far less assuring when I spoke to her over the phone. 'It could be months or even years before everything feels normal again,' she said.

Either way, we were happy to be around one another again and, as she always did, she matched me with a crutch under the arm as we limped through the old town together, past the *pintxos* bars, past the buskers in the plazas, and past the odd brass band bellowing out local folk tunes. Emilio charged up ahead with the disorientation of a calf being led to slaughter, sweating profusely and grumbling to himself as he did his best to navigate the crowds. Eventually we found Tito and

Cecilia sitting in the sun finishing off a bottle of wine. We introduced ourselves, and I was straight away struck by Cecilia's energy. She had a charisma which I found disarming and I could hardly look away from her. We walked along the port, which was bustling with restaurants preparing for their peak lunch service and fishermen trying to flog off whatever goods they hadn't sold earlier that morning, now at half the price. Tourists stopped to take group photos with *Playa de la Concha* as a backdrop and children chased one another along the wharves, spilling ice-cream and tears in equal measure. The sun was high and hot and right for sailing.

'There he is,' beamed Cecilia, her Provençal accent adding music to her aura. 'Ulysses, the best lay in the Atlantic,' she laughed, 'and trust me I've had them all,' she continued, glancing at Tito. 'Haven't I?'

The boat was spectacular and we climbed aboard one by one. Emilio had the hardest time by far crossing the plank, as he admitted to us that he'd never actually been on a boat before. He was about to bail on the adventure just as Cecilia called the captain and first-mate up on deck to introduce themselves. Emilio quickly changed his mind and seemed more at ease as he took in the two rugged sea-men, who could have easily passed for father and son. The younger one took particular notice of Coco, putting out his hand to help her balance, until I butted in and introduced myself as her boyfriend, which was awkward for everyone as Coco and I had never actually had that conversation. She looked at me with hopeful eyes which quickly gave way to sadness, a sadness that said goodbye. Coco was always obsessed with the ends of things, the ends of chapters like in a novel, and it made me wonder if she only kept on living just so one day she could die.

The father and son untied the boat from the wharf as Cecilia let it drift away from port while directing it into harmony with the wind. Then they hoisted the sails and we left the Bay of La Concha, sailing north between the eastern headland and the Island of Santa Clara, saluting our other sea bound companions as we passed them, mostly older couples or families relaxing on a beautifully calm Sunday afternoon. I limped down towards the stern where Cecilia was manoeuvring the rudder and perched myself next to her. The boat was swaying gently in the wind, which made moving all the more difficult for me. Coco and Emilio went down into the cabin to mix drinks while Tito was up by the bow with the father and son as they pointed out landmarks on the shore they recognised. 'I attended a party there once,' I overheard him boast, pointing out a mansion nestled into the rocks. 'Every celebrity who's ever set foot in Spain was there, not excluding the dead. I even had a gin and soda with the ghost of Hemingway.' We continued sailing east towards the fishing village of Pasaia, passing my apartment, the opera house, and the neighbourhood of Gros. I surrendered to the calm of the sea and relaxed at last.

'This is a beautiful boat,' I said to Cecilia, probably a dumb comment but I wasn't sure what else to say.

'Thank you, I love him very much.'

'I thought boats were always a 'she',' I said.

'That is the normal way, yes, but Ulysses is definitely a 'he'. After my husband passed away, being out at sea on this boat was the only way I knew to still feel close to him, to still feel his spirit wrapped around me. Therefore the boat must be a he.'

Her shoulder length hair, grey-blonde, was whipped straight back in the wind, her eyes narrowed into tiny coves which let in just enough light, while her smile was a permanent source of joy across her face, almost ear to ear, with a thousand lines forming elsewhere across her cheeks and forehead as a consequence of its permanence. She had a timelessness about her which only the wind and sea can carve.

'What was your husband like?' I asked.

'Max? He was very handsome and a wonderful sailor, the best I ever knew, but he was not a great communicator. He spoke seven languages and none of them well; even his native Greek suffered. But he spoke the language of the sea fluently, and he taught it to me when I was still young and impressionable, and I've never forgotten it,' her eyes watered up a little.

'When did he pass away?' I asked, perhaps overstepping our acquaintance, but I was captivated by her.

'Over twenty years ago. I've stopped counting, what's the point?' The wind had picked up a little now and the boat gathered pace as it charged towards Pasaia. 'And you,' she turned to me, 'what's happened to you? Why is your leg like this?'

'I fell off a cliff,' I said after a brief pause, choosing to be as honest with her as she was with me.

'How did you manage that?' she laughed.

'I'm not sure. There were no witnesses and I can't remember a thing.'

She looked at me with concern. 'But why were you on a cliff? People don't usually just fall off cliffs.'

'Well I was walking the Camino del Norte,' I started, 'and I was approaching a town named Laredo, and that's where I was found, not far from it.'

She nodded. 'I know the coast off Laredo well,' she said, 'there is a series of small mountains there which are famous for their strong winds, I can see how you would fall up there. It's not the normal Camino path though, I've walked it three times before and I've never gone that way, which is strange.'

'That is strange,' I said, 'I wish I could remember some of it, any of it. I'm sure it was beautiful.'

'It is more than beautiful,' she confided, 'it's tragic. Tragically beautiful. It's possible you were trying to escape the highways, which are very dangerous and ugly and often interfere with the peace, and headed to the coast, and there you slipped. You're lucky to be alive, not many people walk that way—you could have gone weeks without being discovered.'

'I'd like to think that's what happened, but my backpack was at the top of the cliff, which tells me I took it off before I fell, which doesn't make sense. Why would I take my backpack off?'

'So you think you might have jumped?'

'It's a possibility.'

'Do you have any reason to jump off a cliff? Have you ever had any reason to jump off a cliff?'

'God no, the thought of it makes me sick, I've never wanted to stop living, there're too many drinks to be had,' I joked.

'Then you fell,' she said, staring into my eyes. 'Nothing more needs to be said, nothing is simpler, the backpack can be explained a thousand ways. Maybe you stopped to have lunch, stopped to take a photo. There's no reason to keep hurting yourself. I can see that you are full of sadness, but sometimes people fall off cliffs. It can be that simple if you want it to be.'

'Thank you,' I said, eyes downcast.

'Max died by accident,' she professed.

'How?'

'He took a waitress out to sea one evening to make love, off the coast of Crete, and they both drowned in their drunkenness, under a full moon. They were never found.'

'I'm sorry' I said.

'Don't be sorry, I knew the type of man Max was before I'd even kissed with him, it was my choice. I'm just sorry for her, she wouldn't have known. But that's time, it takes the things you love the most and crushes them to dust, nothing lasts forever. Even Ulysses will one day be stripped and used as firewood.'

As she said those words, 'nothing lasts forever,' Coco approached us and sat down next to me.

'What are you guys talking about?' she asked.

'Time,' said Cecilia, 'the cruelty of time,' she smiled.

'Sounds deep,' Coco said, cuddling into my arm. 'I made you both a drink,' she said, handing us each a margarita.

'How did you two meet?' Cecilia asked.

'We made love in the sea,' Coco replied.

I reclined back on my elbows and let my eyes drift between the sea and the sky as I finished off the margarita to the soundtrack of the sails, the waves and the soft conversation Cecilia and Coco were having in French. So she spoke French then? I didn't even know this. As the margarita finished, I unbuttoned my shirt and fell asleep like that. As I slept I dreamt of cliff faces and surging tides and eagles and a town named Laredo I'd never seen before and maybe never would see. In my Laredo the villas all had terracotta tiles and all the tiles had been bombed, maybe from the war or maybe from ETA. I walked the streets of my Laredo searching for Coco. Eventually a girl shouted out my name. She looked like Coco but as I approached, she morphed into Julia, except I still couldn't make out the colour of her eyes. The shouting got louder.

'Artie, Artie!'

Then I woke up; it was Coco, I was still on the boat.

'Artie, lunch is ready,' she said, handing me a plate of fried fish, 'the boys caught it while you were sleeping.'

'The only thing I caught was a cold,' said Emilio, smiling.

'How long was I asleep for?' I asked.

'Long enough for the sun to start setting,' answered Cecilia, as she dug at the food on her plate.

Everyone fell quiet as they ate. The father and son duo sat up front at the bow while the rest of us remained at the stern. The town of Pasaia surrounded us; it was built on a narrow inlet that led from the sea into a natural harbour. The buildings were all wooden, of traditional Basque style and painted different colours—blue houses next to pink next to yellow next to red. A small ferry did a constant loop, transporting people from one side of the town to the other, while fishing boats headed out past us for a night at sea. The sky was blue up top and then orange in the middle and finally pink at the fringes as it caressed the mountains and hills around us which were green and yellow and white. Seagulls and herons did their last dash for an evening snack before settling in for the night, occasionally perching on the boat while ignoring us completely. Emilio sat silently to my right, watching the crowds on the waterfront, perhaps jealous of the camaraderie they showed, something he'd never really known until now. The other three, Tito, Coco and Cecilia, were to my left, fixated with the horizon and the dazzling colours it produced. No one spoke for a long while, enjoying the taste and sustenance of the sea, enjoying the kind of calm which only a sailing boat can inspire. Calm like birth or death or both.

Cecilia spoke first, 'So, Coco, what's your story then?'

'My story is boring,' she said, picking a bone out of the fish on her plate, 'there's not a lot to tell, I'm still a baby.'

'I doubt this,' responded Cecilia, 'I can see myself in you. When I was a young woman, a lifetime ago, I was also running away from something, from everything, and I kept it secret too.'

'What makes you think I'm running away from something?' Coco asked, her face turning serious for a moment, clearly scared of her past being interrogated.

'Why are you here, on a sailing boat with a Spaniard, a Basque, an Australian and a French woman, in a little-known town in a little-known corner of the world? I would say all five of us are running from something, especially Arthur. He remains the biggest mystery to me, because he doesn't even try to hide the fact that he is lost, he accepts it and wallows in it and lets it define him. But why? Maybe we'll never know, maybe it is his purpose to have no purpose,' she was looking at me intimately now, almost seducing me. If Coco wasn't around, I would've gladly leapt into her arms.

'And me?' Tito asked, 'you don't find me mysterious?'

'You, my darling boy, are about as mysterious as a loaf of bread,' Cecilia teased.

'I'm not even insulted,' Tito laughed. 'Bread has its uses.'

'Bread has one use, *mi amor*, to satisfy hunger, and nothing else, much like you.' She leaned across and kissed Tito on the mouth. The rest of us glanced away; Coco and I shared a secret smile.

'What about me?' asked Emilio, entering the conversation for the first time.

'You are beautiful, too beautiful,' Cecilia said, 'and that is mystery enough.'

We continued drinking like that with Cecilia leading the conversation and Tito interjecting every now and then to make us laugh. I was lost in my own thoughts, however, as was Coco lost in hers. What if Cecilia were right, what if I really had no purpose? I'd fled Australia with no plan, and it was almost convenient I got injured, as it allowed me to sit around idly without having to justify it to anyone. I'd lost all ambition long ago. All I cared about now was my next drink, that was enough to satisfy me. But was this just a phase, or was I trapped in a kind of timeless nothingness, just put on earth to consume until my body could consume no more? Consume drinks, food, Tito's cocaine, friends, the tenor's music, the sounds of the sea, the freshly caught fish, the gentle kisses from Coco, the emails from Julia, the sad memories of my childhood, the vitality of Cecilia, the rocking of the waves, the warm-heartedness of Emilio, the pain in my legs, the sleepless nights, the impotence, all of it. And when I was done with all these things I'd fade into nothing, and once the four people who gave me company tonight faded into nothing too would I be remembered at all, would it be as if I had never existed? And what of Coco? What was she running from? Was she a spy or a whore or a child bride looking for a new start, a new name? Surely Coco wasn't her real name, her name would be Sofia or Hannah or something like that. What part did I play in her life? When would she be ready to give me up and run away to somewhere else? Maybe to Corsica or Tangiers or to the mountains in Thailand. When would she no longer need me and when would I no longer need her? I'd need her forever, I decided.

Coco stood up and collected the plates. She headed over to the father and son to ask where to wash them, and the son got up and led her down the hatch to the cabins below. I tried not to pay attention, but it seemed to me that they were down there a very long time together, alone. I started to think that maybe they were making love; that look that the son had given Coco earlier had said 'I want to fuck you,' I was sure, and she seemed to enjoy it. I wanted to go down and see but I couldn't go down the hatch on my own, it was too difficult with my leg. I tried to distract myself and caught Cecilia's eyes. She gave me a knowing look, as if to say 'yes, your girlfriend is down there making love to my shipmate.' I took a sip of wine and put the thoughts out of my mind. About half an hour later Coco returned with flushed cheeks and tussled hair. I ignored her for the rest of the evening and decided I wouldn't accompany the group to Tito's apartment for more drinks after we arrived back in San Sebastian. Instead I sat on the balcony and watched the party through the telescope. This was the beginning of my slow descent into madness. My Act Two.

13

Below my apartment was a convenience store that also sold alcohol and cigarettes, I went inside and grabbed a bottle of Jameson's whiskey and a pouch of tobacco and some filters and papers. I hadn't smoked in years but I felt like smoking tonight. I made my way up the four flights of stairs alone, and by the time I reached my apartment I was physically spent. I unlocked the door, whiskey tucked safely under my right arm, and hobbled in to the living room. I turned the lights on dim and flicked through the tenor's CDs, eventually settling on some flamenco. I opened the shutters to the balcony and a warm sea-breeze flooded the apartment. If there was music on the breeze that night I wouldn't have known, as my own drowned it out. I settled in to a chair and opened the tobacco. I stretched a paper over my fingers and fished out a filter. I pinched the tobacco and sprinkled it out evenly, and even though it'd been a few years, I rolled a perfect cigarette without having to think too much about it. I put it to my lips and then realised I hadn't bought a lighter. I climbed up and grabbed a crutch and wandered into the kitchen, searching the drawers and shelves with no luck. Eventually, ten minutes or so later, I found one amongst the candles Emilio liked to light besides the bathtub. I picked up a couple of the candles and returned to my seat by the balcony, turning out the lights on the way. I lit the candles and then the cigarette and took a healthy swig of whiskey. It sailed through me like musical notes soaring through an organ pipe and my body felt alive again, no longer just the dead weight I'd become accustomed to. I adjusted the telescope and focused it on Tito's apartment. It took me a while to find it in the dark. One by one the lights came on, and as bodies moved through the space, I could pick out Emilio first and after Tito and Cecilia, who were making out against a wall. The balcony lit up as Coco walked out alone. She had a drink in her right hand and leaned against the railing. For five or so minutes she didn't move from her position, and apart from changing the direction of her gaze she didn't really move at all. I wondered if she was searching for me, searching for the madman in the apartment with his two closest friends—whiskey and self-pity—and I wondered if she was sad or angry or both. More bodies arrived in the apartment, Tito obviously having called some friends, and the balcony became crowded. Coco was lost to me amongst the strangers in the dark.

Towards the end of my relationship with Julia I'd been unemployed for several months, having become disillusioned with my career in finance and bored with my life outside it. I wanted to be an artist, I'd tell her. But instead of discovering an inner genius I sat at the local bar and drank until late almost every evening. The alcohol started to infect my brain and I became convinced Julia was having an affair. I started dropping hints to her, the hints became accusations, and instead of defending herself, she just kicked me out of the flat. That sick feeling I had with Julia started coming back now. I recognised it on the boat this afternoon, and the sad part is Coco and I weren't even a serious thing yet, not as far as she was concerned anyhow. We were just a couple of lost travellers who found warmth in one another's arms. For Coco it was temporary, ships passing in the night, but for me it was the only thing keeping me sane, and with each step she took in the other direction my sanity started to crumble. I doubted she'd made love to the deck-hand, I really did, it would have been far too brazen even for her, but I wanted to believe she did in order to be vindicated. I had lost the war with Julia, I wasn't going to lose the war with Coco too, not before I lost my sanity, anyway. I returned to the telescope.

Emilio was on the balcony now, surrounded by a few younger men in sharp suits with cocktails and cigars. He was telling them a story and they were all engaged, laughing and slapping him on the shoulder. It looked as if he'd found his place, if only for a night. To be fair, I had recognised a change in Emilio over the last few weeks. No longer did he seem uptight and by the book. He began dressing more casually, drinking more recklessly and staying at his mother's house an awful lot, which I began to suspect was just a cover for his dates with men. I hadn't brought it up, I was going to wait for him to tell me, but I was sure of it, as more than once his mother had rung the apartment when he was supposedly at hers. By the look of things Emilio would be getting lucky again tonight.

I moved the telescope and could barely make out the kitchen, but I could pick out Tito, his bright green shirt standing out like a beacon, as he leant down over the bench and brought his nose down low to the surface. Next it was Cecilia's turn, and then a hugely overweight woman wearing a pink tutu. I looked around for Coco but couldn't find her anywhere. I took another swig of whiskey and rolled another cigarette. I lit it and dragged it down. It felt good, real good, too good. I put my eye to the telescope again and there she was, always the best-looking girl in the room, except she wasn't alone this time, someone was holding her hand. It took me a second to realise who it was, and then my heart skipped a beat. It was my cousin Javier. The two of them joined Tito at the bench and did a line each.

I pulled back from the telescope and pushed it away. I forced myself up and tripped on the floor as I made my way to the couch, spilling a third of the whiskey in the process. I straightened myself up against the couch, now nicely drunk, and finished what was left in the bottle. I rolled another smoke but passed out before I could light it. I dreamt of nothing, or if I did it was too bleak to remember, too bleak to waste your time with anyhow.

The following morning I woke up in the shower, a garbage bag tied around my right leg, otherwise nude. Emilio was under one arm and a very skinny guy I'd never seen before under the other, the both of them propping me up.

'What the fuck are you doing,' I swore at Emilio, struggling to free myself.

'Washing your own piss off you, you sad little man,' he replied, as he forced my head under the water and I threw up all over them both.

14

'What are we going to do about you, then?' Emilio asked, arms crossed, staring at me with a contempt I didn't know he was capable of.

'You don't have to do anything about me,' I mumbled, the ache in my head pounding away. 'I'm perfectly fine the way I am.'

'You're right, I don't have to, I'm back at the hospital full-time next week so you'll be on your own. But what if I want to?'

'It's fine Emilio, forget about it, forget everything, forget about me. I'm not the problem, Coco's the problem,' I said, smothering my face with a cushion, hiding from the morning light, 'Coco's always been the problem.'

'What makes Coco the problem?'

'Everything.'

'You're making no sense again. You are a strange man Arthur.'

'I saw her with Javier.'

'Last night?'

'Yeah, last night, I watched the party through the telescope like a proper creep. Looked like you all had a real great time without me.'

'But she wasn't with Javier?'

'Bullshit, Emilio, don't lie to me, I saw them holding hands, doing drugs together, it was plain as day. Anyway I don't care anymore.'

'You're right in assuming that's what Javier wanted, but Coco spent the whole night brushing him away. In fact she spent the whole night talking about you. Tito and I could hardly handle it; there is only so much to be said about you, Arthur, but Coco wouldn't know it. The woman loves you and you reject her to wallow in your misery. You surprise me Arthur, I knew you were sad, but I thought it was a beautiful sadness — in Spain we call it *duende*, but this isn't *duende*, this is just pathetic.',

'I don't believe you for a second. Coco loves nothing but herself and even then, she mostly hates herself. But you're a good friend for trying.'

Emilio said nothing and I heard him collect his things and open the door.

'Where are you going?' I asked from beneath the cushion.

'Anywhere, it's not important, anywhere is better than sitting in here listening to you today. Let's go Rico,' he shouted towards his bedroom.

I heard footsteps, and then someone named Rico said goodbye to me, presumably the skinny guy I threw up on in the shower. When the door closed, I was completely alone again. The pounding in my head was getting more insufferable by the second. I tore the cushion away and struggled into the bathroom where there was some pain medication. I took three pills and sat on the toilet with my head in my hands until the pain subsided a little. I looked in the mirror and hell stared back, hell with two empty barrels in place of eyes. I made my way into the living room and thought about calling Coco, but I wasn't exactly sure what I'd say to her and figured she'd just hang up anyway, so I decided not to. Then I decided I needed a walk and ran my head under the tap, willing the water to wash away the rot. I threw on whatever shirt was on my bedroom floor, and made my way down the stairs. About halfway down I got a shooting pain through my leg and I let out a yell and lowered myself in the dark. I felt like crying, I needed to cry, but I just laughed instead. After about fifteen minutes the door on the ground level opened and the stairway light came on. Someone was making their way up towards me. Part of me hoped it was Coco, but I was relieved to see it was just some anonymous neighbour, some old woman with a scarf around her head and a bag of groceries. She kept asking me things in Basque, probably trying to see if I needed help, but I had to explain I didn't speak any Basque, and that I was fine. She helped me to my feet, and I continued down the staircase alone.

Outside the morning air was cold. As a change of

wind brought a draft in from across the sea, it reminded me of Coco and her disdain for the Atlantic. It was a Monday morning and the city was much quieter than it was the day before, although tourists and locals still passed one another in patches down narrow and misty streets. I looked up at the statue of Christ up on top of Mount Urgull and decided I'd make my way up to it, however difficult it would be with my shattered leg, if for no other reason than to take my mind off Coco.

I crossed through the old town, which the machinery of night had just hosed clean after another weekend of summer debauchery. I took a break to have a coffee and a croissant at a café owned by a retired bullfighter from Pamplona and made my way to the port. At the port I took the steps on the right, which led up into the mountain, never stopping to search for our blue and white fishing boat. The path wound around to its northern face and I could see the great expanse of the sea, ripping and roaring to the horizon, merciless and free. I thought about the trip on the boat just twenty-four hours earlier, and how magical it had all been until I decided to ruin it with my jealousy, with my rotten imagination. I also thought of Cecilia and wondered why my uncle didn't just settle down with her. I thought she was probably way too good for him and he knew it too; he could never handle a woman as sure as she was. Continuing around the path I came to a hill with an old cemetery. The graves had been so tarnished by the wind that the names and dates could no longer be read. They were now just blank memorials to an unknown number of forgotten dead, overgrown with weeds and vines which pulled them down towards an indifferent hell. I stopped to rest and have a cigarette, and when it started to softly rain I made my way further up the hill to the cover of a pine forest and decided to wait the rain out. After a while I fell asleep and dreamt of Julia.

She was leading me through a field as eagles swooped us overhead. We were surrounded by grey mountains and green valleys. Then suddenly the earth dropped away all around us and crumbled into a sea, leaving us on a singular pillar above the crashing waves. I reached out for Julia's hand but she pulled it back as an eagle flew down and collected her and stole her away from me. Then I heard a voice and turned, it was Cecilia. 'Jump,' she said, gesturing the edge with her hand, 'why not jump?' So I jumped, and as I fell, I could hear Coco laughing. The further I fell the louder and the more hysterical the laughing got, then I woke up just before I crashed into the waves.

The rain had ceased, or was just a light dusting now, but the clouds had gathered in a huge black mass. It was only 11 a.m. in the morning and the sun was nowhere to be found; the morning had the aura of a winter's evening. I brushed the pine needles off my shoulders and out of my hair and continued up the mountain towards the castle and the statue of Christ. I struggled with the incline, and the crutch under my arm began to burn my armpit, but my leg wasn't in so much pain any longer; the sleep had allowed it to rest somewhat. I took some comfort on a rock for a moment, a few dozen meters shy of the peak, and let my breath catch up. Then I negotiated the final summit and reached the entrance to the castle. I made my way inside. It was practically empty apart from the odd staff member and I took in the view of the city below. To the right was La Concha, the finest beach there ever was, and the newer neighbourhoods which skirted its shore. Directly below was the old town and the historical centre, one of the great old towns of Spain, and to the left was the neighbourhood of Gros and Playa de Zuriola, which had been my home for the last two months. I wondered where Tito might be in that moment; presumably in his apartment recovering from last night's indulgence. Then I wondered what Emilio and his date had decided to do after they left the apartment. I hoped he wasn't too mad. I wondered if Cecilia had returned to sea yet. If she had I wished I had of escaped with her.

I continued around the castle and stared up at Christ, who meant less than nothing to me, and when the rain picked up to what could only be called torrential, I took cover in a small turret, and there I thought of Coco. I didn't want to think of Coco, but I couldn't help myself, because actually, I desperately wanted to think about Coco. I thought of her sad eyes when I ignored her on the boat and how I'd be lucky if I ever saw those sad eyes again. I figured I'd only see distant eyes from now onwards, none of the love, none of the *duende* Emilio spoke of, that spirit which had only ever been Spanish up until that perfect northern European girl harnessed it with her reckless beauty. I also thought of Julia and decided I'd reply to her email. It might actually be nice to see her I thought, especially now that I'd almost certainly ruined things with Coco. Julia could never have *duende*, she was too practical and stubborn for anything of that, but at least she may not hate me.

It was about an hour before the rain finally passed, and on the way down the mountain, I stuck to the path so as not to slip down the hill. It took me almost two hours before I was back in the old town. By now the clouds had split in two and the sun appeared for the first time that day, the soaked streets sparkling like fish in the markets. I stopped at a bar and had three or four beers and watched the crowds as they moved along the street. I noticed a lot more couples than I usually would. Then drunkenly I wandered the town until I found an internet café and logged on to my emails. There was one from my mother, which I replied to first, and then I wrote one to Julia.

Julia,

I'm very sorry, I haven't had internet connection for the last few weeks, it's been difficult for me to do anything to be honest, I've been in a lot of pain and under constant care. I am recovering well enough though, at least that's what the doctors tell me. I'm living in an apartment in San Sebastian with a nurse who looks after me, his name is Emilio and is a real nice guy. My uncle also visits most days. I'll be here for at least another month, so it'd be great to see you, I miss you also. Let me know what date you arrive, and we can catch up; there may even be a space for you in the apartment if Emilio is

*moving out, which I think he might be. The weather here
is crap by the way, bring something warm.
Arthur*

I sent the email and read the news and checked
the rugby scores. I read about the likely nominee for
the Democrats in the USA, some guy named Barack
Obama who was African American, and then I read
about the bombing campaign by ETA. How further
apart could those two countries be right now, I
thought, one is about elect their first black president
and the other is still blowing themselves up. Before I
left I checked the emails once more, Julia had already
replied.

*Arthur,
I arrive Friday.
Julia*

When I got back to the apartment Coco was there
waiting for me.

15

Coco sat alone on the couch beneath the flickering light of the antique chandelier in the stillness of the early evening gloom. The balcony was open wide, and a purple sunset streaked across the walls and gently dusted her profile, highlighting her cheeks, her jaw, her trembling lips.

'How long have you been here?' I asked as I closed the door behind me, closing off the noise and mayhem of the outside world so that Coco and I could find ourselves alone again.

She shrugged and said nothing. She could barely even look at me. It was as if a spell of timidity had been sent to curse her. I leaned my crutch against the couch and moved beside her. Her eyes were downcast, her face turned to stone apart from the fear in her lips. I tried to take her hand, but she pulled it away. There were a thousand miles between us.

'What's wrong?' I asked, trying to make her stir, trying to make her exist.

'Nothing,' she said, 'I just don't feel any good tonight.'

I nodded and said nothing. I understood '*I don't feel any good tonight*,' to mean '*I was with Javier last night and I don't know how to feel about it, I don't know if I should tell you or not.*'

'Why don't you feel good?' I asked.

'Everything just feels cloudy, dark, hopeless.'

I put my arm around her and pulled her in tight. She didn't resist this time, she melted into me.

'I don't feel great either,' I said.

'What did you do last night?'

'I just went straight to sleep,' I lied. 'How was Tito's party?'

'It was fine.'

'Just fine?'

'Yeah, it was ok.'

'Meet anyone interesting?'

'What do you mean?'

'I don't know, did you meet anyone new, anyone you liked?'

'What do you mean '*anyone I liked?*' You sound like a paranoid boyfriend.'

Then she pulled away from me and we both went quiet again. She rested her head on her hand, her lips no longer trembling. She stared out through the balcony doors as the evening descended into night and watched nothing in particular, just the black. She didn't look like herself. Instead of vibrant and youthful she looked worn out and exhausted, as if she hadn't slept a minute, as if she'd spent the whole night wrestling with her demons. Her energy was off too, she was like a ghost, like a damaged reel of film, and I imagined I seemed much the same to her.

'You're probably just coming down,' I reassured her.

'Coming down?' she snapped.

'From the coke.'

'What makes you think I did coke?' she said as she turned to me and glared. I was right, her eyes had lost any affection. 'You were watching me, weren't you?' she continued, 'through that fucking telescope, I knew you would be.' I said nothing and looked away from her. I couldn't handle the fire in her glare, which burnt right through my hopes, my dreams, my everything.

'Would you like a drink?' I asked, climbing to my feet and collecting my crutch. Turning away from her to shield myself.

'Yeah, why not,' she shrugged, 'what else is there to do in this life but fucking drink?'

In the fridge I found a half-empty bottle of vermouth, I poured two glasses over ice and cut two orange slices and threw them in. I returned to the living room and found Coco fast asleep, curled over the arm of the couch as the small of her back rose gently in the glow of lights emanating from the promenade below. I poured her glass into mine and sat down beside her with my hand caressing her forehead. Outside I could hear some music coming from a concert by the beach. It was a pianist playing something soft and gentle, magical even, which turned the moment into something out of a film. I finished the vermouth and faded towards sleep myself, there in the dark with Coco under my arm. At some unknown hour she woke up.

'Arthur?' she said softly, a tiny tremor in her voice.

'Yeah?' I asked as my eyes adjusted themselves.

'How long was I sleeping?'

'I have no idea. It's completely quiet outside so it must be late.'

'Were you asleep too?'

'Yeah, I was.'

'Oh, I'm sorry I woke you.'

'It's ok.'

'Should we go climb into bed?'

'I don't mind, I'm comfortable here.'

'Me too.'

'I'm glad you're with me Coco.'

'Me too. Arthur?'

'Coco?'

'Are you in love with me?'

'Probably, if not right now then soon. Are you in love with me?'

'I'd like to be.'

'I'll take that, that's good enough for me. Let's go somewhere nice, just the two of us, tomorrow, a trip somewhere.'

'How? Neither of us can drive.'

'Well we'll get the train.'

'Where do you want to go?'

'Somewhere in the mountains, I'd love to be alone with you in some tiny village in the mountains.'

'Ok, we better sleep some more then. I'll call in sick to work tomorrow morning.'

'Goodnight Coco,' I whispered, in what must have been the darkest night I'd ever known.

'Night, Artie,' she echoed back. I could still hear the pianist in my head.

Tito had a friend who owned a mountain cottage outside of a town named Aragües del Porto, which was about 200kms southeast of San Sebastian in the Spanish Pyrenees Mountains. We left at midday on a train to Pamplona, passing countless vineyards along the way, and then took a bus east along the mountains towards the village. The trip itself took about four hours all up, with Coco fixed to the window, watching the world fly by outside as I stole glances of her, glad for us to be alone together.

When we got off the bus we were caught off guard by the cold, which neither of us had dressed for, and jumped straight into a cab. We didn't bother to explore the town, preferring to go straight to the house and worry about the rest later. We were tired as all hell. It was an old cottage, made of mossy stones and ancient wooden beams and supposedly built in the sixteenth century. Inside it was charming and slightly more modern, but it really felt like we'd gone back in time to the only time this town had ever known. As soon as we arrived, Coco started collecting firewood from under the house and lit a strong and thirsty fire in the living room. I poured us each a glass of wine and we curled up in front of the flames together, about as content as you'd ever find us.

'I'm from Belgium,' she said, breaking the hypnotic grip of silence which had coated our afternoon, 'I'm tired of playing games with you Arthur.'

'I figured you were,' I replied, 'when you started speaking French to Cecilia. I connected the dots well enough, I'm not entirely useless.'

'Clever boy. So you can understand French then?'

'No, not at all.'

'You're terrible at languages,' she laughed as she elbowed me in the ribs.

'Most Australians are,' I admitted, 'it's not the same in Australia, languages aren't as important as they are here.'

'That's stupid. Why do so many Australians come to Spain then?'

'Have you looked around the forest here Coco, what trees do you notice?'

'Pine trees? Why?'

'Ok, apart from pine trees?'

'I don't know? Why do you ask such stupid things? This is why I hate you, everything you say is stupid.'

I climbed to my feet and got my crutch, 'Follow me,' I said, 'the fire will be fine without us.'

Coco got up and followed me outside the cottage, it was already late afternoon and the air had a frosty sting to it and it felt good on my skin and good to breath. It had rained a little earlier in the day and everything was still wet. I led her down the steps and along the driveway until we found an ancient path that escaped the street and slithered down a hilltop and deep into the forest. All around us the trees were wiry and phantom-like and covered in moss. Birds and but-terflies flirted with one another as they darted across our way. It was getting dark now, with so many leaves above us, hiding us from whatever light was left in the sky. I led the way, using the crutch to swipe away at the cobwebs that were everywhere ahead of me. At one point we came across an old fountain and we paused to drink from its spout. The water was fresh and clean and rejuvenating. A frog watched on for a moment before leaping into the mossy pool. Beyond the fountain in the overgrowth were the remains of what looked like a bombed-out hamlet, almost out of view and almost certainly out of memory.

'What do you think happened there?' Coco asked, gesturing towards the ruins.

'It was probably bombed during the war,' I said, 'both sides bombed buildings indiscriminately, not caring who they killed, although the fascists were much crueler.'

'The World War?' she asked.

'No, before the Second World War the Spanish had a civil war; five hundred thousand died. But it was kind of like the Second World War because the Nazis and the Italians and the Russians were all here. It was also like a proxy war for fascism and communism, although that isn't fair because it was also uniquely Spanish. Either way you look at it it was horrible.'

'Why do you know so much about it?' she asked.

'My grandfather fought in it, so I've read some books.'

'What side did he fight on?'

'The fascists. He was a fascist,' I admitted, 'it's hard for me to say that but I'm told he didn't have much of a choice.'

'I see,' she said, 'don't feel bad about it, my grandfather was a Nazi too, it's not our fault.' She moved closer to me, eager to share the warmth of her body. 'Is this what you wanted to show me?'

'No, not at all, I didn't even know this was here. Let's keep going,' I said as I led her down a little further until I found what I was looking for. 'Ok, look around you, what trees do you see, apart from pine trees?'

She took a minute or so to survey the canopy above and the leaves underfoot. 'Is it called eucalyptus?' she asked.

'Yes, exactly, eucalyptus, and eucalypts are Australian. A long time ago, Catholic monks from Spain visited Australia to spread their faith, and finding the climate similar, they brought back eucalyptus seeds to create plantation forests, and the trees spread like wildfire across most of the country. The trees just seemed to belong here, like it was a second home, and Australian people are the same. There is something about Spain that makes Australians feel like we belong, that's why there are so many Australians here.'

Coco stared at me and said nothing and for a moment I couldn't read her thoughts, and then she laughed, a slow giggle that snowballed into something more hysterical. 'You brought me all the way out into this cold, wet forest, when I was so happy and warm in front of the fire, to tell me this stupid story?' she kept on laughing. 'It is the dumbest story I've ever heard.'

'I'm sorry,' I said, genuinely trying to defend myself, 'I thought it was interesting that so many …'

'Come here,' she demanded, cutting me off sharp as she grabbed the back of my head and pulled me in close for a kiss, our first real kiss in days. 'You know what I want to do?' she asked.

'What?'

Instead of using words she slowly moved her hands down towards my belt, then she got to her knees and lowered my jeans. There underneath the silent gaze of that tall and mighty eucalyptus forest, was the closest thing to making love that Coco and I had managed since we had reunited after my accident. If anyone else were in that forest that afternoon we wouldn't have known, we wouldn't have cared, we cared just for one another and our strange and inexplicable love. When we returned home we rebuilt the fire and then showered together. We spent the rest of the evening curled up by the warmth, each of us trying to understand the other while giving nothing away ourselves.

'I still don't understand why you're here,' she said. 'You make no sense.'

'I understand nothing about you, I know you're from Belgium and that's it. Do you have a family?'

'I don't want to talk about that.'

'Why are you running away? Are you a spy?'

'If I was I couldn't tell you, obviously, so I suppose I am. Spying on stupid Australians for the Belgian government. What if I told you I'm a diamond thief?'

'I'd probably believe you to be honest, it'd make a lot of sense.'

'Well I'm not, but I could be, I could just be lying to you again.'

'What do you mean again?'

'Don't be so insecure, Artie. And why are you running away? Are you a murderer?'

'If you thought I was a murderer you wouldn't be here.'

'You don't know that, you see, that's what pisses me off about you Arthur, you assume everything. Maybe I like being the lover of a murderer, maybe it turns me on, or maybe I am a murderer myself, you wouldn't know, you'll never know anything.'

'What's your surname?'

'It's a secret.'

'What's your real name?'

'It's also a secret.'

'When will you let yourself fall in love with me?'

'I won't, Arthur. You know this, don't make it more difficult for yourself. When will you forget about me?'

'As soon as I possibly can.'

'Good, you'll forget me the day I'm gone then.'

'I was lying, Coco, I'll never forget you, and I'll never let you go anyhow.'

'It's cute to me that you think you have a choice in what I do. Are all Australian men so controlling?'

'I don't control you, Coco, at least I don't mean to. Why can't you be nice to me?'

'I'm not nice to you when I suck your dick?'

'That's different and you know it. You're intent on hurting me, whether it's now or next week or next year. You know you'll do it because you want to do it.'

'I'll do it, Arthur, because I have to do it.'

'But why?'

'Because everyone has a past, and some people have a past they can't escape. Aren't you meant to be a traveller? How can you be a traveller and know so little about people?'

'How can you be so beautiful and still be such a cunt?' I asked.

She leaned in and kissed me. 'We have tonight, no? Maybe it should be our last night? Our last goodbye?'

'Let's not use words like last and goodbye,' I said. 'Actually, let's just not use words.'

We curled into one another and slept like that on the floor in front of the fire, never having disturbed the covers on the bed in the room behind us. In the morning we woke up in much the same position. The fire was out, and a chill ran through my body.

'Last night was sweet,' Coco said.

'Last night was a tragedy,' I responded.

'But don't you know, Arthur, I only like tragedies.'

The town was a beautifully preserved example of medieval Spain. We walked around the streets and visited the church and took some photos in front of the mountains and with some donkeys behind an old wooden fence. The day grew hot and stifling, the polar opposite to the brisk afternoon we enjoyed yesterday. After walking along the stream and searching for trout, we decided to stop for some *tapas* and a few beers. We ordered *chorizo*, ox-tail and *patatas bravas*, and I ate most of it while Coco sat there and laughed at me.

'I've never seen someone eat this way,' she joked,

gesturing her fork like a shovel. As the food was almost finished, I noticed a breaking news story on the television above the bar. I pointed it out to her.

'Do you know anything about these guys?' I asked.

'Is it ETA?' she responded, doing her best to translate the Spanish at the bottom of the screen.

'Yes, what's it say?'

She translated it for me. 'Three bombs in the south of Spain have gone off, no one injured so far but ten thousand evacuated. Wow, it's lucky no one was hurt.'

'It's been happening all summer,' I said, 'it's a real shit situation.'

'Sometimes my language students make jokes that they will join ETA and I'm never sure if I should report them to the head teacher or not. They are just children after all.'

'You probably should,' I said, 'it's these young minds they prey on. I think my cousin might have something to do with them.'

'Your cousin? You mean the one who was at Tito's party?'

'Javier, yeah. I'm not sure, it's just some comments he made a few times.'

'That's strange,' she said.

'I agree, he isn't even Basque, his dad is from Madrid and his mother from Valencia.'

'That doesn't matter,' Coco replied, 'he was born here after all, he is allowed to identify as Basque. Besides, he was really nice.'

'You thought so?'

'Yeah, handsome too. But don't worry, you're

much more handsome.' She leaned across and kissed me. 'But if he's a terrorist then he should be in prison.'

'I'm not saying he's a terrorist,' I said, taking a sip of my beer, 'it was just some comments he made, it made me think he might be.'

'Weird. He invited me to learn surfing at his school near San Sebastian. I said yes but maybe I should change my mind.'

'You do whatever makes you happy, Coco, I'm not here to control you.'

'Good boy, people have tried before and it didn't end well for them,' she said with a wink. We caught the late bus back to Pamplona and the evening train home, Coco slept the whole way as I glanced from the window to her, back to the window and back to her for the entire journey. Willing it to never end.

16

A few days later Emilio burst in to my room before I had a chance to shake my hangover, 'Guess what!?' he shouted, pulling me awake by my better leg. I'd been fast asleep and had no idea what was happening.

'Emilio,' I murmured through the early morning daze, 'what the hell are you doing, what time is it?'

'Eight in the morning, now guess what?' he continued, wide-eyed like a lunatic.

'I'm not ok with you just barging in like this,' I said, 'how do you know I wasn't naked or something.'

'Seriously, Arthur? I'm your nurse, I've seen your dick more times than I've seen my own.'

'Only because your gut makes yours invisible,' I snapped as I blocked out the light from the living room with a pillow over my face.

He moved his hands up and grabbed my leg at the

ankle and the knee, 'Want me to break it again?' he asked as he twisted it against the natural direction.

'Ouch!' I shouted, trying to kick him away, 'Alright I'm sorry, I'm sorry, let go. Let me get up and go to the bathroom and then you can tell me everything.'

'Deal,' he said, leaving the room, 'today is a good day Artie!'.

I mustered all the effort I could and got myself up and went to the toilet. I brushed my teeth and spat out black phlegm and had a quick shower, doing my best to keep the right leg dry, but getting it fairly wet anyhow. Being able to shower myself was just about the most exciting thing that'd happened to me lately, apart from Coco of course. The shower was small and awkward and it made for a comical struggle when Emilio had to jump in and help me out. I looked in the mirror, and for the first time in months I thought I looked ok. The greys were still in the beard and my eyes still revealed my alcoholism, but these were my permanent imperfections, they were going nowhere, and yet there was a positivity in my eyes which I'd never seen before. I felt good and happy and strong and I figured it probably had a lot to do with the trip that Coco and I had taken together. I was sad for it to have ended and I honestly could have moved out to that little cottage with her and got some dead-end job in town and lived out my days like that perfectly happily. She'd probably get bored, I thought, yet if she was on the run from something, which I was starting to think she definitely was, there'd be no way they'd ever find her in a one-bedroom cottage in Aragües del Porto, a bygone town in the

Spanish Pyrenees that time and all its travellers had forgotten. We'd be perfectly anonymous to everyone except each other, it'd just be Coco and me and the donkeys and the long nights by the fire and the love-making in the eucalyptus forest by the bombed out ruins.

I threw on whatever shirt I saw first and pulled on some tracksuit pants. I walked out into the living room and found Emilio standing in the middle of the floor with two flutes of champagne.

'Do you always take such long showers?' he snapped at me through his boyish grin.

'I thought that was pretty quick,' I lied. He handed me a champagne. 'No, Emilio,' I protested, 'it's nine in the goddamn morning, aren't you meant to be a nurse?'

'In Spain, we say '*Salud!*'' he said, raising the glass.

'*Salud!*' I responded, taking a sip and finding it quite good. 'So, don't keep me in suspense any longer, what's the news?'

'As you'll remember my audition for Tito's friends in Bilbao was yesterday,' he started.

'Ah yes, of course,' I said, when in reality I'd forgotten all about it.

'I've had my "friend" Rico,' he gestured the inverted commas on friend, 'work with me over the last few days on a few monologues, one by the great Spaniard, Calderon de la Barca, one in English by William Shakespeare and one by the masterful Russian playwright, Anton Chekhov, which we translated into Spanish. I arrived in Bilbao early, much earlier than I needed to, and felt like a nervous fool, an absolute fake, and decided I'd visit the Guggenheim for some inspiration. I spent two hours in there amongst Picasso and Miro and Gaugin and it worked. I arrived at the theatre right on time, introduced myself to the panel and knocked it out of the park for six, as you Aussies say. This morning I got a phone call to say they are hoping to use me for a production of Chekhov's *The Seagull* in November, playing the doctor, Dorn. Arthur, I'll finally be an actor, and I owe it all to you!'

He leapt over to me and gave me a huge hug. I tried to adjust my leg before he crushed it, but I didn't manage and the pain was excruciating.

'Emilio, that's fantastic,' I congratulated him through the agony, 'I'm so happy for you, tonight we have to celebrate.'

'No, Arthur, tonight we must destroy ourselves,' he declared as he pulled away from me. 'You call your uncle and your lady and I'll organise Rico. Drinks are on me tonight, Arthur.'

'Well they gotta be on someone,' I said beneath my breath.

Tito arranged for a table for us in a place called Ganbara in the old town of San Sebastian. It was more a bar than a restaurant, with the entire bar-top covered in elaborate and brightly coloured *pintxos*, most of which were made from ingredients of the sea. It was packed full of people on a perfectly warm Saturday evening, but we managed to get a table way up the back anyhow as the owner was a friend of Tito's, like everyone else in town. We were treated like royalty from the moment we arrived, and we toasted to Emilio, whom we made our king for the evening, and who had spent the afternoon reading and re-reading *The Seagull* and even highlighting his lines.

'Emilio,' Tito shouted across the table, 'how about a monologue, entertain us for your meal!'

Emilio immediately went as red as the *albondigas* on his fork and started protesting. 'Tito,' he said, 'I'm shocked, you of all people must understand that an actor is an artist, delicate like the last flower in spring, and not some monkey who will perform for you at dinner parties with the click of a finger.' Everyone laughed.

'This is where you're mistaken my friend,' Tito responded, 'an actor is just a piece of meat, designed to shut up when not on camera and make money for the producer and little else,' he teased, while Cecilia jabbed him in the ribs. 'Cecilia is elbowing me now to make me stop but it's true, why do you think I gave it up? So I could finally use my brain and make some serious cash, not just collect the scraps off the floor at film festivals.'

'Bullshit,' Emilio countered as he got to his feet, 'an actor is the vessel through which we see our own lives, our own experiences, our own fears and hopes and dreams, and from the actor we learn how to deal with our own adversity and rise above it!'

'You say bullshit,' Tito continued, 'but I say double bullshit to that. The writer puts the words in the actor's mouth and the director tells the actor where to stand and all they must do is try not look too ugly or mumble! But enough of this conversation, I can already see our friends are becoming bored and it is too easy for me to win.' He raised his glass: 'To Emilio, the dancing monkey, and to the beginning of his journey, his journey towards the realisation that Tito Ramiro Ramirez is always right.'

The waiters started filling the table with *tapas* and *pintxos* as we ordered more wine and got down to the serious business of drinking and eating. Cecilia was just across the table from Coco and me, and we took the opportunity to ask about her travels. All the while Coco kept her right hand under the table, massaging the inner part of my thigh.

'The furthest I've ever sailed?' Cecilia repeated, trying to remember. 'Probably New Zealand, I think that's the furthest I've ever been. Circumnavigated both islands with just two crew members, then we settled in to Milford Sound for a couple of months. On the way back to Europe we stopped in to Sydney for a week. It rained the whole time though, so I didn't think much of it unfortunately. It was much more exciting up north of Australia, where we anchored off a place called Cape Tribulation. Have you been?'

I shook my head as I took a mouthful of calamari.

'Well you must go, it's very beautiful, one of my favourite places.'

'What's your absolute favourite?' Coco asked.

'Oh that's easy, Cuba, it's as if you've disappeared sixty years into the past, the buildings and coastline are so beautiful, and the people are very beautiful too,' she said, 'I always imagined I'd marry a Cuban man.'

'My father was Cuban,' Tito interjected.

'Ok,' Cecilia conceded, 'maybe I'll change my mind then, Cuban men are out!'

'And where do you want to go the most?' Coco asked.

'Antarctica,' she said, without taking a moment to decide. 'I am going later this year, maybe even next month, it depends if I can organise a crew in time.'

'Amazing,' I said, 'I'd love to visit somewhere like that, somewhere empty and desolate.'

'You can,' she said, shrugging her shoulders in the same way Coco would, 'if your leg is fixed why not join me?'

I turned to Coco, 'Want to go to Antarctica together?' I asked.

She smiled and looked as if she were about to say yes, but then her eyes went sad and she said nothing.

I was about to ask Cecelia about the logistics of sailing to Antarctica when someone approached us, someone whom nobody at the table but myself could possibly recognise. Her hair was straight and brown, and I was finally able to know the colour of her eyes—green, but completely unremarkable, unlike Coco's blue and grey ones, which were as remarkable as anything I'd ever seen.

'Hi, Arthur,' Julia said. 'nice of you to reply to my last email.'

I lowered my fork to the plate as Coco withdrew her hand and placed it on the table, I took a quick swig of wine and sort of half stood up, half sat back down, and half stood up again.

'Um,' I stalled, not sure what to say next, 'everyone, this is Julia, an old friend from Australia.' I saw a flicker of betrayal in her eyes when I chose the word friend. 'Julia,' I continued, 'this is everyone.'

Tito stood up first to introduce himself and then I introduced her to Cecilia, Emilio and Rico. When I got to Coco Julia's eyes narrowed.

'I didn't know you had a girlfriend,' she said.

Before I could say anything Coco interjected, 'Oh, I'm not his girlfriend, we're just friends.' Hearing her say it like that, as cold and calculating as anything she'd ever said, felt like a knockout kick from a mule.

'Coco and I are just keeping it casual,' I added, trying to spare myself the embarrassment of the moment. Coco glared up at me and for the first time Julia smiled.

'Would you like to join us?' Tito asked, ignoring my unease.

'I'm not sure I'm invited,' Julia said, 'besides, I'm hanging out with some people from the hostel, but thanks.' She started to leave and then turned around and locked eyes with me, 'If you want to catch up sometime, Arthur, I'm here for a while, just email. If not, I don't care. Nice to meet you Coco,' she added before she left.

'Who was she?' asked Rico, once Julia was out of sight and lost in the crowd.

'That was an ex-girlfriend, I completely forgot she was coming to Spain. What are the chances of her running into us?'

'You didn't tell me anything about an ex-girlfriend being here,' Coco said.

'I'm sorry,' I said, 'as I said I put it to the back of my mind. She hasn't meant anything to me for a long time and I just forgot. Besides I told her not to come; couldn't you see how uncomfortable she made me?'

'Oh well,' Tito said, trying to get the two of us to move on from the bitter intrusion, 'all's well that ends well, right? Now, who wants some cocaine?'

'Me!' Coco said with an alarming enthusiasm as she pushed past my broken body and followed my uncle into the bathroom. Cecilia looked at me displeased, somehow I had managed to spoil the night and I had no idea how.

17

When I awoke the following morning I couldn't see a thing. The room was as black as the haze of regret which flowed from some deep spring inside of me. Not a single source of light could be discerned as I fumbled around in the dark like an invalid. I had no idea of where I was or who I was. Eventually I landed on my feet and allowed myself a moment's pause before I reached around and felt the bed, the bed stand, the lamp. I began to understand, I was in my bedroom, safe in my bedroom. I stood up on broken and uneasy legs and shuffled my way to the ensuite door. I reached inside and flicked on a light which blinded me at first before settling in to a warm orange glow. My eyes adjusted and I could see my way through the bedroom now. I headed past the bed and made my way to the door. As I entered the living room a gust of wind blew a chill right through me, the balcony doors had been left wide open and a draft was coming in. Outside it was dead quiet; the tireless rumble of the sea was the only noise interrupting an otherwise dead night, but even the sea was not its usual self. I went into the kitchen and checked the clock on the oven. It was 3:27 in the morning. My mouth tasted like a half-drunk beer repurposed as an ashtray and my teeth stuck to the back of my lips. I tried to coat them with saliva but there was none, my mouth was void of any liquid at all. I poured myself some water from the tap and took a drink, and then I closed my eyes and tried to gain control over the rhythmic thumping in my skull, but it did nothing to ease the pain. I made my way to the bathroom and pissed for what felt like an hour and then got some pain killers from the cabinet and took the usual three. I sat on the toilet until they kicked in and poured myself some more water. I felt like crying or dying or both.

I tried to make sense of the situation and replayed the night in my mind like a video cassette in rewind. I had a somewhat vague memory of an argument with Coco on the street outside Ganbara. I had no idea what the fight was over, but it was vicious. I could remember leaving the bar and Emilio following after me. I remember I was very drunk, really very drunk, as I had done numerous shots on my own up at the bar after the encounter with Julia, which had left me shaken. On the walk home I convinced Emilio to have one more drink and there I did another shot while he was finding a place to sit. Then I have no more memories, just black. I figured Emilio probably came home with me but when I entered the living room I noticed his door was wide open. I walked over and took a look; the bed was strewn with various bits of clothing but no bodies, I was alone.

I headed over to close the balcony doors and glanced over at Tito's apartment. It was a roll of the dice, but I had to see, and sure enough the lights were on and there were bodies moving through the space, not too many, just a few. I tried to resist the urge to look but I couldn't, so I rolled a cigarette and sat in front of the telescope and adjusted it until I could see clearly. I lit the cigarette and settled in for another session of masochistic bliss.

The first person I could make out was Tito, shirt unbuttoned, holding court with some epic from his past while all around hung off every word. Emilio was sitting on Rico's lap, stroking the back of his neck while managing to get a word in every now and then. Cecilia sat back in her chair with a glass of wine in her lap, eyes almost closed but refusing to retire just yet, half listening and half daydreaming the way she always was. The table was predictably strewn with drinks and drugs, I reached up and fingered my own nostril. It was powdery and dry. Coco sat opposite Tito, eyes wide, the most awake of them all, by far the most enthralled in whatever fanciful story Tito was relaying to them, probably some bullshit about a mistress with ties to royalty. Behind her stood Javier, his hands gently massaging her shoulders, he bent at the hips and whispered something to her ear. I pulled away.

The blood rushed to my head like a torrent in a stream, I took a deep, dark drag of the cigarette and stood up and reached for the phone. I rang Tito's number and watched. At first no one budged, then Tito got up and answered.

'Hola?' he said.

I said nothing, careful not even to breathe.

'Hola!?' he repeated.

I hung up.

I let the telescope drop and closed the balcony doors and made my way back to the bedroom. I was furious not just at Coco for being intimate with Javier but at my friends who sat around the table and happily let it happen, perhaps they were justified though, maybe they were all filthy at me for spoiling the evening somehow and saw this as nothing less than what I deserved. But how could they tolerate Javier? The guy was a snake. Eventually, after the painkillers had kicked in and I felt alright again, I let my body crash into the bed and fell asleep without having to try too hard.

I was physically and emotionally exhausted, but I couldn't even find peace in my sleep. Instead I dreamt of Coco and Javier, wearing ETA insignia on their clothes, conspiring to blow up a town named Laredo. I tried to stop them, but I fell off a cliff. Then they blew up the town and everybody laughed.

18

On Playa Zurriola there was a little beach bar which was constructed every year in the weeks leading up to summer and deconstructed in the weeks leading up to winter. I'd often watch it from my balcony through the telescope and get jealous of the people drinking there, enjoying the sun on their face and the sand between their toes. Now, finally, I was one of those people as I downed a mojito while waiting for Tito to meet me.

After crashing out in the morning I woke up around midday and got in touch with my uncle. I had a need to understand what, if anything, was happening between Coco and Javier and I figured he was the most likely to cough up the truth. He admired honesty more than anything and despite all his flaws he was a mostly honest man. He said he'd meet me at two, and it was now two forty-five, which for my uncle was not unusual, and I was quite content to wait for him so long as I had a drink. Suddenly a hand gripped me on the shoulder, and I spun around.

'Sorry I'm late, Artie, I was held up with phone calls, need a drink?'

'Sure,' I said as I surveyed the contents of my glass, 'another mojito would be great.'.

He returned a few minutes later with a mojito and a beer. 'What a glorious day,' he sighed. And it was, the day was indeed glorious. After a somewhat patchy summer, which was now in its final twenty-four hours, it seemed as if the best weather had been saved for last. The sky was a perfect blue, a deep and vibrant ultra-marine up above and soft and silky along the horizon. Seagulls streaked across it, their shadows scooting along the sand. It felt about twenty-eight degrees and the beach was as packed as I'd seen it all year. I wanted to swim but I was still unable to, in truth I was happy enough just being amongst it at all.

'I'm too old for this, Artie, these all-night parties, way too old,' he confided.

'I don't know how you do it to be honest.'

'It used to be easy, now it's an uphill battle. I should have gone home with you.'

'When did I leave?' I asked sheepishly.

'You don't remember? Of course you don't, you were a wreck. You left just after midnight, disappeared like a ghost with Emilio, after you and Coco had an argument outside.'

'Do you know why?'

'Yeah, she was annoyed at you for not having

mentioned Julia, I tried to tell her it was an accident, but she knew it wasn't. It's a tricky spot you're in.'

'It isn't really,' I said, 'Julia means nothing to me, and Coco means everything, it couldn't be simpler. Why do you think Julia was so pissed at me? Because I've been ignoring her emails for weeks.'

'Well Coco wasn't buying it. Maybe you should introduce the two of them properly, and show Coco more affection, treat her like the princess of the two. That should make things pretty clear.'

'You're right, I'll do it tonight.' I made a mental note to send Julia an email once I left the beach and then call Coco. 'How's your speech going?' I asked, 'have you started yet?'

'Are you kidding?' he responded. 'I haven't even written the first line and it's less than three weeks away now.'

'Let me know if you need some help writing it, I've got nothing but free time.'

'Thanks, Artie,' he said, finishing his beer, 'I'll need all the help I can get.' He gestured the empty bottle, 'Another?' he asked.

'Sure,' I responded, 'just a beer though.'

While he was gone, I watched the surfers catch waves way out past the breaks and I felt contempt for them, a jealous hatred stemming from the image I couldn't erase from my mind, Javier stroking Coco while leaning in to whisper something to her. What was he whispering, I wondered? *'Let's go back to mine, we can have more fun there'* or *'I can't believe you were ever with my cousin, that guy is pathetic.'* A surfer was walking towards me from the sea, his board under his right arm and his wet-suit pulled down and dangling from his hips. His body was chiseled like a wild-cat and his eyes shone with the spirit of perfect freedom. How could I ever compete with that? How could Coco choose me over Javier? Regardless of how psychotic he could seem at times I'm sure he was charming as all hell to her. I couldn't even have sex with her properly. When Tito returned I brought it up.

'Tito, can I ask you something?'

'Of course you can, what's up?'

'I woke up around three in the morning, and I went to close the balcony doors and then I noticed the lights on in your apartment, so I looked through the telescope.'

He laughed, 'I figured you'd be doing that, you have to come join us next time Artie, it's really a lot of fun.'

'I want to, I mean I will, for sure, next time. But I noticed something last night which made me feel kind of shit.'

'What was that?'

'Coco was sitting at the table and Javier was kind of massaging her; it looked pretty intimate although I couldn't be sure.'

'Yeah, I noticed that too,' he said. 'To be honest with you I think he's pretty keen on her, and every time you and her have an argument it probably pushes her away from you a bit, in fact I know it does, she told me so.'

'Really? She told you that?'

'Yeah, she did. I think she has some hang-ups around men not trusting her, controlling her, something in her past I suppose, although you know what Coco's like, every little thing is just another secret.'

'So you think she might be into Javier as well?'

'I have no idea, after last night I really don't know.'

'What happened last night?'

'Nothing that I saw, but they left together around four, he was probably just walking her home.'

I went quiet for a moment. My worst fears had been confirmed, Coco and Javier were seeing each other. 'I'm surprised he keeps popping up at your place,' I said. 'I didn't think you guys were on very good terms.'

'He's my son, Artie, what the hell am I supposed to do, disown him? Anyway, when there's a girl around who he's keen on he tends to behave himself pretty well, in fact it's just about the only time I can tolerate him.'

'I see,' I said.

'Look, Artie, I can tell you're down about all of this, but it's no good talking to me. Invite her out tonight and invite Julia too so she can put that insecurity to bed. Coco is the only one who can answer your questions, not me and not Javi. You know what he wants, it's up to you to show her you're the better guy. Which you are,' he said, rubbing my shoulder, 'a thousand times better.'

I thanked him and we finished our beers together before he left. On the way home I emailed Julia, who agreed to meet, and called Coco, who reluctantly said ok after taking a lifetime to answer the call. Then I went home and tried to make myself look human again, which was an almost impossible task on this final day of summer.

At 6 p.m. I sat alone in the Plaza de la Constitucion, waiting for Julia to arrive. It was a warm evening and hundreds of people moved around me as I sipped on a bourbon. I had spent the rest of the day listening to music and sketching in a pad I'd found in Emilio's room. I wasn't much of an artist, but I was desperate to do anything which would keep my mind off Javier and Coco. I was enjoying myself now in the plaza, and to be honest, I was disappointed when Julia turned up. I'd been quite content to sit there with my drink and my thoughts and watch the crowds go about their business alone.

'Hey,' she said, pulling a chair out and sitting opposite me, 'this place was hard to find.'

'Was it?' I asked, 'It's the biggest plaza in San Sebastian. I thought it would have been easy.'

'Yeah but this city is like a maze, nothing is easy here. Did you order me a drink?'

'No, I wasn't sure what you'd want.'

'You know what I drink.'

'I do?'

She shook her head in disappointment and called over a waiter. She ordered a glass of sauvignon blanc; something I should have known, apparently.

'So, what's the plan tonight?' she asked.

'Well Coco will be here in half an hour or so, I thought we could just eat here and catch up or go somewhere else if you'd prefer.'

'Coco is joining us?'

'Is that a problem?'

'I guess not, but you should have told me. Is Coco her real name?'

'I'm not sure, but it's the name she likes, so what's it matter?'

'Fair enough.'

The waiter brought over the wine and neither of us said anything to each other for a while. It was a lively evening in the plaza and there was plenty to distract us both from having to talk. I regretted the night already, although the waiter was charming.

'So, what's your plan, Arthur?'

'Sorry?'

'Your plan, your life plan, what is it?'

'Plan? I don't have a plan. Why do I need a plan?'

'Because you're going to turn thirty soon, Arthur, and you'll have done nothing with your life.'

'Wow, that's nice of you to say.'

'It's true, isn't it? What have you achieved?'

'I've done a lot, I've travelled, I've finished university, I've taken care of my mother. Do you ever have anything positive to say?'

'Don't get defensive, Arthur, I'm trying to help you, someone has to.'

'Why? Why do you have a problem with what I'm doing here? I don't ask anything of anyone, I keep to myself.'

'And that's the kind of life you want?'

'What if it is?'

'It's weird, Arthur, it's really fucking weird. What's your ambition? What will you do for work?'

'I don't know, Julia. I'm recovering right now; in case you've forgotten, I fell off a cliff not too long ago. I'm not thinking of work, that's the least of my worries, and ambition sounds like a dirty word to me right now.'

'And what about your mum? You say you care for her and yet you abandon her in Australia alone?'

'My mother didn't even recognise me last time I visited the hospital. She has all the care she needs.'

'And what about me?'

'Excuse me?'

'So you just forget about me that easily?'

Before I could respond to Julia I saw Coco walking through the plaza. She was wearing blue denim jeans and a faded denim jacket over a black top. She approached the table slowly, almost reluctantly. I stood up to greet her and she turned her cheek when I leaned in for a kiss. The moment wasn't lost on Julia.

'Coco, you remember Julia,' I said, gesturing towards her.

'Hi,' Coco said as she took a seat.

'Hi,' said Julia.

'Would you like a drink?' I asked, she nodded, and without asking what, I ordered her a glass of *tempranillo*. Julia threw me a terrifying look.

'How do you like San Sebastian?' Coco asked.

'It's really nice,' Julia replied, 'the food is really random though.'

'What do you mean by random?'

'You don't know what random means? Like, strange,' Julia said.

'You mean the *pintxos*?' Coco asked.

'I'm pretty sure it's called *tapas*,' Julia replied.

'Actually it's mostly *pintxos* here,' Coco corrected her, 'the little bites of food on the bar, I love them, I think they're great.'

'Whatever they're called I don't like them. I can't stand seafood.'

We all fell quiet, no one knowing what to say or why we were even there. The waiter brought Coco's wine to the table and I ordered a beer.

'So, what do you do Coco?'

'Not a lot,' she said, sipping the wine, 'I'm doing some shifts in a café and I teach English sometimes.'

'Really? You can teach English when it's not your language?'

'I've spoken English since I first started speaking, so it kind of is my language. Do you speak any other languages?'

'Me? No chance. I find them really boring. The only languages you need in Australia are English and Chinese,' she laughed. 'So you and Arthur must have a lot of free time together since you guys don't really do much,' she added.

'Coco works a lot actually,' I butted in, 'she's just being modest.'

'You don't have to answer for me, Arthur,' Coco said as Julia laughed. 'I keep pretty busy, I have some projects I work on at home.'

'Like what?' Julia asked.

'Oh, just personal stuff, but it keeps me busy.'

'Sounds mysterious,' Julia said.

'And what about you?' Coco asked, 'What do you do back home, apart from not learn languages?'

'I'm an investment banker actually, been doing it for five years, moved up pretty high in my company actually.'

'Sounds exciting,' said Coco.

'It is,' she continued, 'especially when you start making the kind of money I do, it's really exciting.'

'I'm not the type of person who finds money exciting, I prefer adventure, experience, you know what I mean? Or maybe you don't?'

For a while Julia said nothing, instead she just stared at Coco and smiled. 'You know, Coco,' she said, 'is that even your real name?'

'It's the name I use, so I suppose it's real enough.'

'It sounds like a stripper's name to be honest.'

'You think so?' Coco asked, 'That's funny because there's nothing Arthur enjoys more than watching me strip.'

'That's cute. Anyway, you know Coco, you might think your life here is pretty amazing, inspiring even, but wait until you're fifty, I think you're gonna be a pretty miserable woman, and it sounds like you're dragging Arthur down with you.'

I went to cut Julia off but before I could Coco had stood up and turned to face me. 'Thanks for a lovely evening, Arthur, just like last night, you're really on a roll right now. Julia, if you're making so much money, why do you wear fake diamonds? Those earrings are really pathetic, or are you just making it all up to impress yourself? Enjoy your evenings. Don't bother calling me again, Arthur.'

She turned from the table and walked off into the plaza, I wanted to follow her, but I knew she'd brush me away, I knew this was the end that she always spoke of, and what a sorry end it turned out to be.

'She didn't even leave money for her drink,' Julia sniped. 'What a bitch.'

'Oh fuck off, Julia, you were horrible just then.'

'Fuck you Arthur,' she said, rising to her feet, 'this whole stupid evening was your stupid fucking idea. And now your little girlfriend has left you, how pathetic. At the start of the night I wouldn't have believed you could be any sadder than you already were, and now looking at you I just laugh, I can't believe I wasted two years on a loser like you.'

'You're ugly, Julia, inside and out but especially inside. You should leave San Sebastian, this town doesn't suit you.'

'You know what suits you?' she asked.

'What?'

'White wine,' she yelled as she threw the contents of her glass into my face. 'I hope your little stripper never calls you again, loser.'

She stormed off away from me and I watched her fade out of my life for good. I looked towards the direction Coco had vanished and she too was nowhere to be seen. The waiter came up to me and offered me his towel.

'Would you like the cheque, *señor*?' he asked.

'No,' I said, 'not the cheque, just another beer please, and maybe a shot.'

'As you like,' he said, 'as you like.'

I sat back in the chair and wiped my face clean. A few of the tables around me were still staring and I threw them a look. The waiter returned and I did the shot.

'The night is young,' he said, 'and it seems you are definitely alone now. Would you like some recommendations?' he asked

'Please,' I replied, 'anywhere, anywhere dark and loud, the type of place a person can disappear in.'

'I know just the place,' he said, 'you'll be perfectly anonymous.'

I finished the beer and left him a tip.

19

I rolled over and felt a body, a naked body with the sheets pulled down to the small of her back, breathing gently and not making a sound. The light was soft from the courtyard window and it caressed her skin with a yellow morning glow. Still half asleep and probably still drunk, I figured it was Coco, until I ran my hand along her back and up to where her hair began, which was dark brown instead of blonde. My next thought was it must be Julia, and I pulled my hand away. I tried to replay the evening in my head, but I couldn't, there was nothing. All I could remember was after leaving the table in the plaza I went on a kind of pub crawl through the old town, drinking heavily at each stop. At some point, I supposed, I ran into Julia and invited her back here. We were both naked, so I thought it safe to assume the worst.

'Julia' I said hesitantly, 'you awake?'

She stirred and mumbled something as she came out of her sleep.

'Julia?' I repeated.

She rolled over to face me. It wasn't Julia.

'Julia?' she said, 'Are you serious? It's Georgina. Get it right.' Then she rested her head back on the pillow and closed her eyes. 'Although,' she continued, 'to be fair I have absolutely no idea what your name is,' she laughed.

'Arthur,' I said, staring blankly at the ceiling, 'my name's Arthur.'

'Cute name,' she said quietly, 'never met an Arthur before.'

'Do you remember much of last night?' I asked.

'Not really, although I remember you had a pretty hard time dancing with that leg of yours,' she laughed.

'Please tell me I wasn't dancing.'

'Oh don't worry, you weren't dancing,' she laughed again, 'but you were trying.'

'What time did we come back here?'

'I don't know,' she replied, 'I tried to get you to come to mine but you said you had cigarettes, and we sat on your balcony smoking for a while. Then we had sex.'

'We did?'

'Yeah,' she said, 'clearly you didn't enjoy it as much as I did.'

'You enjoyed it?'

'Of course. Are you always this self-conscious the morning after?'

'I just feel bad because I can't remember much.

Where are you from?' I asked.

'London. And you're an Aussie, yeah?'

'Yeah, I'm an Aussie.'

She sat up now to face me, the sheet falling away from her and revealing everything. She was beautiful. 'Since you can't remember last night,' she leant down now to kiss me, 'let's try again.'

After Georgina and I had sex again, the first real sex I'd been able to perform since the accident, I got up from the bed and had a shower. The last forty-eight hours had seemed like a complete disaster, nothing had gone right, and now it seemed like it was all beyond repair. I longed hopelessly to be back in the village alone with Coco, sitting by the fire, sharing stories about our pasts while revealing absolutely nothing. Not only had Julia and I destroyed any chance of a friendship moving forward, but Tito had confirmed my worst fears about Coco and Javier, while Coco herself seemed to want nothing to do with me. And to make it all the more difficult to deal with, Emilio had moved out to stay with friends in Bilbao while he began rehearsals for *The Seagull*. I'd never felt more alone, although Georgina seemed cool.

I took a longer shower than usual, finding the hot water too comforting to quit, and made myself look as good as I could before returning to the bedroom where Georgina was. When I entered the room she was already dressed.

'You take really long showers,' she said.

'Yeah, I've been told.'

'Hey while you were in there a girl came in the

room and gave me these,' she said as she handed me a set of keys. 'She said she won't be needing them anymore.'

'Did she tell you her name?'

'Nope, she didn't really say anything, I think she was a bit embarrassed just walking in and finding me naked on the bed, I also thought it was a bit weird to be honest.'

'What'd she look like?'

'Blonde, blue eyes, sounded French.'

'Coco,' I said to myself.

'What?' Georgina asked.

'It was Coco. Do you know if she left?' I was kicking clothes around the floor now, looking for a shirt to put on, I found a blue and grey flannelette and buttoned it up.

'Yeah, she said to say goodbye.'

'I'm sorry, Georgina, but I've got to go, it was nice to meet you. Stay as long as you like.'

'Good luck with Coco,' she called after me as I charged out of the apartment.

Down on the street I hurried as fast as I could to the plaza where we had watched the acoustic guitarist a few weeks back, which was the first time she promised me it was all going to end. I looked around but couldn't see her anywhere and continued through the old town in the direction of the apartment she was staying in. She'd only showed me her apartment once before, but I managed to locate the door anyhow. The street was already filling with people and I looked like a total mess, wearing the flannelette shirt and grey tracksuit pants with wet hair and a crutch under my right arm. I buzzed apartment 1 and was quickly told in Spanish to go away. I tried apartment 2 and there was no answer. Then I tried apartment 3 and someone responded, it seemed to be an old woman.

'*Hola?*' she said.

'*Hola,*' I replied, '*hablar Ingles?*'

'No,' she said sharply, '*no Ingles.*'

'Coco,' I said, '*Coco aqui?*'

There was a pause, then I heard her shout 'Coco!' in the background. After a moment Coco came to the intercom and spoke to me.

'Hello,' she said softly.

'Coco, it's Artie.'

'What do you want?'

'To say I'm sorry.'

'What are you sorry for?'

'That girl this morning, I don't even know her.'

'It's fine Artie, you can have other lovers.'

'No I can't.'

'Why not? I do.'

'You do?'

'Look, Artie, I don't want to have this chat, things got out of hand really quickly, I wasn't ready for anything like this.'

'But I love you, Coco.'

'You don't Artie, if you loved me you wouldn't be mad with me every second night, you wouldn't try to shape me into your ideal woman.'

'Please, Coco, can I come up and talk?'

'No, Artie, no way. I need to go now, and you do

too. I'm leaving town for a while, but I'll get in touch if I come back.'

'What do you mean if?'

'I told you in the village that that should have been our goodbye, how much nicer was that than this? But you didn't want to listen to me, you never listened to me, so now this is our goodbye, right opposite the bar we met in. Take care, Artie.'

Then she left the intercom and I was alone. I looked behind me and she was right, it was the bar we had met in. A whole summer had gone by since. I backed away from the door and reluctantly made my way home, part of me hoping Georgina would still be there although I wasn't sure why. When I got back in the apartment there was a note from her, I scrunched it up without reading it and threw it behind the couch. I needed Coco, no-one else.

20

It was an entire week before anyone else showed up at the house. I spent Monday evening drunk and alone, reliving the night Coco and I had met, reliving the evening we reunited, reliving the escape to the mountain village and the stroll through the forest and finally reliving the call on her intercom outside the bar where we had met. It had gone full circle and she predicted it all, it was as if she staged the whole thing. She was the girl with the faraway look in her eyes, running from a past she kept under lock and key. If only I'd listened to her, maybe I could have saved it. She gave me enough chances, but I didn't, of course not.

Tuesday morning I woke up on the armchair in the living room. The doors to the balcony were wide open and a cold breeze had made its home in the apartment. Next to me were the victims of last night's massacre

—a dozen beers, two bottles of wine and whatever was left in a whiskey bottle I found under the kitchen sink. It could have been turpentine and I wouldn't have known. I felt like hell and my whole body ached, particularly my leg, although my head was almost as bad. None of this stopped me from embarking down the four flights of stairs, out to the street and up to the bottle shop, where I bought so much alcohol I had to do two trips back to the apartment in order to carry it. I used a credit card Tito had left me, which I hoped he didn't follow too closely, although by now I didn't really care if he did.

Around 8 p.m. on Tuesday, blind drunk, I called Coco's apartment. The old lady who I'd spoken to the day before told me in broken English that she'd already left. I asked where and she said to stay with a friend in Zarautz, but she wouldn't tell me which friend. The only person Coco knew in Zarautz, as far as I was aware anyhow, was Javier, and so I pulled the phone off the wall and threw it behind the couch. Then I settled in to drink solidly but I passed out before I could give it a real shot. When I woke up on Wednesday I was well and truly sick, both physically and mentally but mostly physically.

For all of Wednesday, Thursday, Friday and the entire weekend, I didn't leave my bedroom. Instead I stayed under the covers with the whiskey and the cigarettes within reach and slept as much as I possibly could. Occasionally, when I was awake and sober enough to have thoughts, which wasn't often, I'd think over all the things Julia had said to me in the plaza that evening. She was right, I had no plan, and I had no intention of ever having a plan. I tried to think what I might like to do with my life, but nothing stood out as particularly exciting or even possible anymore. I was almost thirty, as she said, and I wasn't what you'd call equipped with skills to enter the workforce. These thoughts were dragging me down deeper and deeper into a well of misery and so I took a huge swig of whiskey and knocked myself out. I kept this pattern up until a buzz at the door woke me early one morning. I had no idea what day it was. I answered the intercom in my underwear.

'Yeah?' I said.

'Artie? Is that you?' the voice responded.

'Yeah, who's this?' I asked.

'Emilio, you want to let me up?'

'Don't you have a key?'

'Coco has my key, are you going to let me up or not?'

'Yeah, um, yeah of course, hold on,' I responded, fiddling with the intercom until I heard the door open.

I looked around the house, it was as if a bomb had hit it. There were empty bottles strewn everywhere and makeshift ashtrays beside every possible seat. Cigarette butts were scattered on the floor like dying cockroaches. The one thing missing were scraps of food and it occurred to me that I hadn't eaten once all week. I looked in the mirror and I looked like a soldier returning from the front, malnourished and dead in the eyes. The only endearing feature was a full and flowing beard which was hiding half my face. There was no way I'd be able to fix the apartment in a hurry, so I decided not to bother trying and I sat there and waited for Emilio on the couch. When he arrived he was wearing a coat and a scarf and he looked physically spent. He hated climbing stairs; he was a heavy man and stairs were the enemy.

'Artie, it's freezing out there, those winds are insane,' he said, entering the room and closing the door behind him.

'Yeah, the town really sucks when it's like this.'

He took a look around the apartment. He didn't even try to hide his dismay. 'Artie, what the hell has happened?'

'Oh, this?' I said, gesturing the mess, 'this is nothing, just a couple of nights inside, you know how it goes.'

'This is more than a couple of nights, please tell me you at least had help.'

'Yeah, my three buddies, Me, Myself and I, we had a great time, partied like it was the end of the world. Just because summer is over it doesn't mean the good times have to end. Want a drink? I think there's still a half-drunk beer floating in the toilet.'

He walked over to me and put his palm to my forehead, 'Artie you've got a fever,' he sniffed the air in the apartment, looked at the butts on the floor. 'Have you been smoking?'

'Yeah, I started last week, figured we're all gonna die sometime so why not speed it up a little.'

'Ok, you need help,' he said as he walked over the where the phone used to be, then he paused. 'Artie, where's the phone?'

I gestured to the area behind the couch. He gave me a look like I'd just killed someone, then he got his mobile out of his bag. He rang someone and had a conversation in Spanish while I closed my eyes to take control of the pain.

'Alright, Artie, I've just withdrawn from my rehearsals for the next two days. I'm staying here and getting you back in shape. Now tell me, what the hell happened?'

'Nothing happened, I'm just enjoying my holiday, don't you know I'm from Australia and I'm supposed to be on holidays here, you don't need to worry about me.'

He came and sat right next to me and grabbed me by the chin, turning my head so I was facing him, 'Artie, enough bullshit. Don't forget I used to be a nurse and will be again after this show. I've spent my whole life helping people out of shit situations now tell me what's wrong.'

'Nothing is wrong,' I replied.

'Arthur!' he snapped.

'Everything is fine,' I muttered.

'Where's your uncle?'

'I don't know,' I said, 'haven't heard from him all week, he's probably doing cocaine off a stripper's ass somewhere.'

'Where's Coco?'

'Screwing my cousin in Zarautz.'

'Excuse me?'

'You heard me right, and don't pretend you didn't know about it, I saw you all sitting around the table at

Tito's, Javier all over her, none of you saying a damn thing to stop it, forgetting I ever existed.'

'It was your choice not to be there those nights Artie, and you had made a real mess of things every time the two of you got together. The poor girl just wanted to love you and you kept screwing it up.'

'The girl just wanted to do lines and fuck, didn't matter who with, and unfortunately, after I tried to kill myself, neither of those things are very good for me anymore.'

'Tried to kill yourself? I thought we decided you *fell* off that cliff.'

'How do you just fall off a cliff Emilio! Think about it. You wanna know something? Just this morning I was thinking this apartment is just high enough to kill me, almost zero chance of survival from that balcony, must be higher than that stupid cliff I chose last time. If only there'd been a bigger one.'

'I don't like you talking like this Artie,' he said. 'I don't like it at all.'

'Well, Emilio, I don't really give a shit what you think, you're just a nurse, not a friend, and I didn't ask for your opinion. Stay here if you want but I'm going to bed.'

I left Emilio in the living room and crawled into bed, feeling more alone than I ever had before and hating myself for the way I'd spoken to him. He had my best interests at heart, which was foreign territory for me, and I pushed him away so I could feel like myself again. Next to the bed was about a fifth of whiskey, just enough to drown out the day I figured, and I downed the whole lot in one go. That afternoon I didn't dream, dreams were beyond me now, there was just black, black all around, which is where I had decided was the best place to be if I was to keep on living.

21

The following morning, which began as dark as the previous night, came quickly enough. I stood by the balcony with the doors wide open and looked out past the horizon. The ocean, hardly visible through the heavy fog of rain which had settled in over the bay, was cold, distant and cruel. It was no longer a friend, indeed far from it, like all else it was an enemy now. Down below me there was no-one on the street except the garbage men doing their 6 o'clock run and the occasional pilgrim heading westward along the shore, westward towards Laredo, optimistic about what would likely be a doomed journey, doomed like my own. The surrounding hills could just be discerned rising above the horizon, almost black and almost invisible and almost comforting. I heard a door creak open behind me, slowly. Purposefully slowly.

'Artie?' Emilio asked, a tremor in his voice, 'Is everything ok?'

'Everything's ok,' I said, 'everything *is* ok. Why shouldn't it be?'

'Why are you on the balcony?' he continued, as he silently made his way closer to me, inch by agonising inch.

'I'm just watching the world go by,' I said, 'I've been hiding from it all week, all month. Sometimes I think I've been hiding from it my whole life. I wanted to see if it's really as scary as I'd imagined it to be.'

'And is it?'

'Maybe, I'm not sure. It looks cruel today, very cruel, but maybe that's just its mood this morning, or my mood, who can tell. It looks content at least, like it knows who it is, which is more than I can say.'

'It's ok to not know who you are.' He was beside me now, calm, also watching the rain. 'I've been hiding from myself my whole life.'

'But now you are free, you know who you are, you are no longer afraid. Was it worth the wait?'

'I don't know for certain, but it has to be, right? What other option do we have?'

I looked down to the cold, hard pavement below. Emilio followed my gaze, 'That, I suppose, that is our other option,' I said.

'But what kind of option is it? You told me your father went that way, did it do him any good?'

'Not that I know of, certainly not with the living, quite the opposite.'

He hesitated a moment and then said, 'Jumping won't bring Coco back.'

'Nothing will bring Coco back,' I replied, turning to him, 'Coco is nothing now, not in my life, she can't be.'

'That might be true, but there'll be another Coco.'

'You're lying to me again, how can you know that?'

'Because I am older than you, and I've spent my whole life with heartbroken people, and one of the things I've learnt is that another always comes along. Why and how, who knows, they are the mysteries, but the fact remains that another always comes along.'

'What if I don't want another?'

'Then write about her, sing about her, become the next Chekhov and create plays about her, learn the guitar and play songs about the *duende* which she has cursed you to carry on living with. Sail the seven seas and tell every drunken pair of ears in every ungodly port about her golden hair and blue eyes and strange tattoo at the nape of her neck. Spell her name out in the stars, Coco, it won't be hard, it's only four letters, spell it drunk above the Greek islands with a young lover who doesn't even speak your language. Use her, do what you must, abuse her even. Surely any of that is better than to jump.'

'You're right,' I said, stepping back from the edge, the edge that was my home, 'and I'm sorry for everything I said last night.' I gave him a hug and felt like crying, but of course I couldn't.

'It's ok, Artie, I've known you long enough to understand that you only ever mean half the things you say.'

'But which half, how can you tell?'

'You're a good person and not a very good liar, so it isn't hard."

Emilio left me alone at the balcony and made his way into the kitchen, I could hear him filling up the kettle and setting two mugs on the counter.

'Artie, I had a thought,' he called out to me.

'What's that?' I shouted back.

'Let's go for a drive.'

'When?'

'Today, right now, well after this coffee anyway.'

'Right now? But the weather is hell.'

'It won't be a problem,' he said.

'How do you know?'

'Because it only rains day and night in the Basque country, and we're off to Cantabria.'

'Cantabria? What's in Cantabria?' I asked.

'Oh, not a hell of a lot, just a little town called Laredo, heard of it?'

We drove west from San Sebastian along a highway that twisted and turned through pasturelands of cows with bells and rolling green hills. From time to time the road would hug the coast and I'd stare silently out the window, watching the jagged cliff faces and violent waves flash by and think of nothing but Coco. I imagined her running beside the car, begging us to pull over, trying in vain to keep up with us, constantly falling behind and then constantly catching up again. Eventually, when the signs started to indicate a turn off for Zarautz, I lost her for good and turned my attention away. I blocked her from my mind and started up a conversation with Emilio.

'Have you ever walked the Camino?' I asked, as he sped along the shiny, empty road, no other cars ahead or behind, it was us alone, two free and lonely pilgrims on a highway.

'No, I never had the time, if I wasn't working, I was caring for my parents. I would like to one day though.'

'It's very special,' I said.

'How the hell would you know?' he asked. 'You don't remember a single day of it.'

'True. But looking out the window right now, at this scenery, it must really be something. It has to be.'

'You're probably right. How did you hear about it anyway?' he asked.

'Some people in my hostel were planning on doing it, and I asked them a lot of questions. I had no real plans, so I went out and bought some proper boots and decided I'd try it, if I didn't like it after a week I'd quit.'

'How long did you end up lasting?'

'Just over a week actually, and then I quit, although far more dramatically then I'd planned.'

'When your leg recovers, you should finish.'

'I was thinking that just now, I probably will. It'll be the first thing I've ever seen through if I manage to.'

By now Zarautz, and therefore Coco and Javier, were well behind us. We approached Bilbao as the highway became congested and uninspired and we moved along slowly. Eventually we left Bilbao, having driven around the city instead of through it, and we passed through a town called Portugalete. I saw something that made me make Emilio stop the car.

'What's wrong?' he asked.

'That bridge,' I said, gesturing a grey iron bridge that carried what looked like a giant bus without wheels across a river via suspension ropes. It looked like something out of a dystopian science-fiction film or a steam-punk horror.

'I recognise that bridge.'

'Maybe you've seen a photo of it? It's quite famous,' he said.

'No, I've never seen a photo of it, not at all, but I can remember riding across it in that suspended car.'

'And?'

'And? Don't you get it? My memory might be coming back. If I can remember that bridge then maybe I can remember everything else.'

'Ah, I see,' he said, 'then let's stop.'

Emilio parked the car and we got out and bought tickets to ride across the river again on the suspended bus. I paused after we got off and I admitted that no new memories had come back, although I knew for certain I'd been there before. On the other side we stopped and had a beer in a waterfront café.

'Do you recognise anything else?'

'No nothing, just that bridge.'

'You want to know the story of it?'

'Sure, why not?' I said, taking a sip. The afternoon was warm, and the sun broke through the clouds and landed on my face. I began to feel something akin to happiness again.

'In Spanish it's known as the Puente de Vizcaya, in English the Bridge of the Basques. It was designed by an architect named Palacio who was a student of Gustav Eiffel. During the Civil War, which condemned the Basque country to an unimaginable hell, it was bombed and almost completely destroyed. From his house up on the hill,' he turned, gesturing at the neighbourhood that rose steeply behind us, 'Palacio, now an old man, watched his masterpiece get destroyed.'

'What did he do?' I asked.

'He died, what else could he do?' Emilio responded.

'Of what?'

'A broken heart I suppose.'

'That's tragic,' I said, not sure what else I could say. There were a million stories like this across Spain and a billion more across the planet.

'Yes of course, but they rebuilt it and today it is a famous heritage site, so it sort of has a happy ending.'

'I suppose it does, a legacy at least'

'Let's see if you too have a legacy,' he said, downing the last of his beer. We got in the car and continued driving.

The next major town we drove through was a place called Castro-Urdiales, which was another I had walked through on the Camino, according to my passport, although it didn't seem particularly familiar to me. We passed a sign on the highway—Laredo—it was less than 20 kilometres away.

'What do you want to do once we get there?' I asked, 'Explore the town? Relax on the beach?'

'We're meeting someone for lunch.'

'Who? A friend of yours?'

'A friend of mine?' he laughed, 'Certainly not, a friend of yours though, yes.'

'What do you mean a friend of mine? I don't know anyone in Laredo,' I said.

'I know you don't, but he knows you, very well.'

We never actually reached Laredo; instead we turned off towards a small town named Liendo, which was a little further inland and a little further east. It was very small, a few dozen cottages and a church and not a hell of a lot else.

'So, who is it then?' I asked, getting out of the car.

'His name is Fonsu,' Emilio replied, surveying a hand-drawn map he'd sketched out over the coffee earlier that morning. 'You'll just have to sit there though, he doesn't speak a word of English.'

'And what does Fonsu do?'

'Fonsu is a shepherd, or was a shepherd, I think he had to stop just recently.'

Fonsu's cottage was very small and made of stone. The driveway led down to the front of the structure, which was a room elevated on stilts with age-old stairs leading up to a broken wooden door, while under it was a dark and open shelter, presumably for animals to take cover in in poor weather or winter or both. To the right of this was a tall green gate that led to a small cobblestoned courtyard full of brightly flowering plants in brightly coloured pots. Before Fonsu came out to greet us, I had already counted no less than seven cats, all young and healthy-looking and basking in the sun, not knowing how fortunate they were that the dark and moody skies of the Basques had not yet stretched their arms this far west to Cantabria.

Fonsu was a small man, not even reaching my sternum at full height, who had big, calloused workman's hands, shaped out of the hardships of the land, and long, industrious feet gifted to him by his Basque heritage. He had a large nose, perfect for sniffing out the weak amongst his flock, and giant flag-like ears, packed full of long white hairs, which had seen more winters than any olive bush in the valley. When he smiled, a toothless gummy smile, disgusting to the eye but pleasing to the soul, his eyes smiled too, almost closing, almost disappearing under gigantic folded eyebrows. He wore a green checked shirt, tucked in to yellow linen trousers that were supported by thinning suspenders and a black beret, which I had thought exclusive to the Basque Country, but apparently a fashion choice that had crossed the border into Cantabria too. He introduced himself, taking my hand in both of his, and greeted me in *Castellano*, then he introduced himself to Emilio and led us into a garden, where we sat at a white plastic table under the shade of a plum tree in full bloom. He returned inside to fetch two bottles of local cider and three small glasses, while a feeble black and white kitten, eyes half closed with pus, leapt onto my lap and quickly fell asleep. The day was warm and sunny and Fonsu's garden radiated an energy of peace and tranquility and perfect otherness. An otherness far removed from the bitterness which had infested my apartment by the sea. The kitten purred gently as Fonsu uncorked the bottle of cider, raised it high above his head with his right arm, lowered a glass with his left arm and poured the cider from a great height, about eighty percent of it landing in the glass and the other twenty splashing onto the grass beneath his feet. He placed it in front of me and filled up the other two in the same fashion. Then he sat down opposite, his huge and awesome smile never flinching while Emilio thanked him for the hospitality. We raised our glasses, said '*salud,*' and took a sip. The cider was brisk and bitter but utterly refreshing and the day took on a magical hue, almost spiritual, as I looked around the garden and admired the trees, flowers, vegetables and cats. Coco, the girl from the blue and white boat, was far from my thoughts for the first time in weeks.

Emilio and Fonsu spoke for a long while as I sat there and listened, stroking the kitten which remained asleep in my lap. At first, mostly just Fonsu spoke, his eyebrows raising and falling to lend exclamations to his story, which, as it progressed, became more and more animated, reaching a crescendo with him standing on his stool and waving his arms wildly in the air like a madman on stilts. I tried to pick out words here and there, but his accent was thick Cantabrian and his toothless mouth mumbled as if he were chewing an exotic toffee. Even Emilio had to focus in order to understand him. After a while, Fonsu slowed down and Emilio started to ask some questions, and finally the monologue was allowed to become a conversation. I went to refill my cider, being the only one who was taking the time to actually drink it, but Fonsu stood up and took the bottle from me. Emilio explained only a skilled pourer was allowed to refill a glass of cider, and Fonsu went through the same ritual as before and then sat down and continued the conversation. The sunlight sifted through the leaves of the plum tree and over my face. I closed my eyes and stopped trying to understand them anymore. What the hell was the point? After a while I fell asleep and dreamt of Fonsu, staring down at me from the top of a cliff, reaching out his hand, which was always an inch or two too far. I kept trying to grasp it and it kept on slipping. Suddenly a different hand shook me and I woke up, I was alone with Emilio. The sun on my face had begun to retreat and Fonsu was nowhere to be seen.

'Was I asleep long?' I asked.

'Not that long,' he said. 'I was thinking how I'd like to join you.'

'It is the perfect day for a siesta.' I replied. 'Where's Fonsu gone?'

'He's inside preparing lunch.'

'OK. What'd he say?'

'You need to know now, or I can tell you later?'

'Why not now?'

'I think he has more to add.'

'Alright, save it for later then. Was he annoyed that I don't speak any Spanish?'

'No, in fact he was annoyed at himself for not speaking any English, but he is a shepherd, he would never have gone to school, so what choice did he have?'

Fonsu returned to the garden from the house and carried a large silver platter of barbecued lamb and fried potatoes. He placed it on the table and did another trip to gather some plates and a garden salad. He said something in Spanish and gestured at the food.

'This lamb was his favourite,' Emilio said, 'it was almost a pet. He was saving him for a special occasion, so you should count yourself lucky.'

'Well, we'll have to make sure there's nothing left then, won't we?' I replied, not sure if they were joking or not.

I hadn't eaten all week and the food was delicious, although my mouth had taken such a beating from the cigarettes that I found it hard to chew. After lunch there was more cider and Fonsu went inside again and returned with an antique-looking acoustic guitar.

'He'd like to play some music for us,' Emilio said, 'he learnt how to play this guitar during the war, when he fell in love with a beautiful gypsy girl from Andalucia whom his parents were hiding from the fascists.'

Fonsu propped the guitar on his lap and hung his head low as all expression faded from his face, then the fingers on his left hand began dancing along the strings on the neck of the instrument while the fingers on his right hand flicked away at the strings on the body. The music was sweet and haunting and devastating all at once. I stared vacantly at the garden, imagining his Andalucian gypsy girl dancing under the apple tree as a young Fonsu serenaded her. Or perhaps she serenaded him as he danced. Emilio sat with his eyes closed, his head swaying rhythmically with the rises and fall of the flamenco. Fonsu kept his hung low, only raising it occasionally to sigh or let out a call of gypsy despair, and when he allowed himself, a stream of tears escaped his mournful eyes. He continued like this for the better part of an hour, until, as if struck by lightning or taken out by a bomb, he finished with a violent, furious flourish that made the hair on the back of my neck stand up. Emilio jumped to his feet.

'Bravo,' he said, clapping enthusiastically, 'bravo! You see Arthur, this is *duende*, this is what I spoke of, the beautiful sadness which only the Spanish and the Basques can understand.'

'It was magical,' I said, 'I've never heard anything like it. Can you ask him what happened to the girl though?'

Emilio translated the question into Spanish as he sat back down. Fonsu turned and stared at me, his eyes betraying an impossible melancholy, and he said simply, in perfect English, 'They chased her into the hills and shot her.' He wiped away his tears and laid the guitar to rest.

22

After lunch we cleared the table and washed the plates and climbed into the car. Fonsu directed us to a small beach nearby named Playa de Sonabia, a nudist beach, and quite busy today. To the west of us was a mountain peak, which Fonsu explained was named *Ojo del Diablo*, the Eye of the Devil.

'That's where we're headed,' Emilio said, 'if it gets too tough Artie, let me know and we'll turn back.'

'I think I'll be fine,' I said, 'so long as we take it slowly and there's not too much climbing.'

'There's some climbing,' Emilio said, 'but I'll help you up.'

'Let's do it then,' I said, and we began our ascent with Fonsu leading from the front.

The first hundred metres up from the beach were a shallow incline, which I didn't find difficult at all, apart from the great heat of the sun which was near impossible to escape. Fonsu bounced off the stones as if he were a goat, which was understandable, as he must have walked this path a thousand times since his childhood. Approaching a plateau beneath the peak of *Ojo del Diablo*, the path became steep, and Emilio had to stay close behind me, occasionally lifting me up to meet a ledge I couldn't negotiate alone. The edge of the path fell off into a sharp cliff, which was overgrown with small, thorny bushes and tumbled off into the roaring sea far below. We were a few hundred metres up now.

After about an hour or two of climbing we came to a clearing, which was the last place to rest before the final ascent. Emilio and Fonsu had a conversation while I admired the view. The vast expanse of ocean and perfect blue sky surrounded me, only occasionally interrupted by a giant Cantabrian eagle flying closely overhead, checking to see if we were predators or prey.

'This is as high as we go,' Emilio said.

'We're not heading to the peak?' I asked.

'Fonsu explained that if you were on the *Camino*, and intended to reach Laredo, there'd be no reason for you to go any higher than this, instead you would have continued westward along this path here,' he said, gesturing a narrow path along the hilltops.

'Let's continue then. I don't like my chances of making it up there anyway.'

'I don't like my chances either,' Emilio conceded, still trying to catch his breath.

The next section of the walk was flat and easy as we crossed rolling green hills, which were covered in sparse vegetation, wild native grass. Fonsu, as always, was far ahead, and he stopped at a place where the path moved close to the edge and hugged another cliff face. As we approached, I noticed some rope fixed to the cliff where the path became particularly narrow and dangerous; at one point it was barely a foot wide.

'Recognise anything?' Emilio asked.

'No,' I said, 'not specifically, although…' I trailed off.

'Although what?'

'I've seen this place before, definitely, I've seen it many times.'

'So you do remember?'

'No, I don't remember anything actually, but I've seen it in my dreams. In fact all my dreams are here, every dream I've had lately. This is the place isn't it?'

Emilio nodded as Fonsu watched on, trying to understand a word here and there.

'This is where Fonsu found you,' Emilio said, 'your bag was right there where you are standing now. He thought it strange a bag would be lying here and no one around, so he looked over the cliff face and there you were.'

'Can I take a look?' I asked.

'Of course, that's why we're here, but I'm going to hold you.'

Emilio moved in next to me and gripped me by the belt while holding the rope fixed to cliff with his other hand. I lent slightly over the edge and peered down. Below me, about fifteen metres or so, was a small ledge about three metres across and five metres deep. Below the ledge the cliff fell about seventy-five metres further before vanishing into the sea, which was wild and furious at its base. I gripped Emilio's hand and pulled away from the edge.

'So I was on that ledge then?'

'Correct,' Emilio said, nodding.

'What does he think happened?' I asked.

'He told me at lunch that when he found your bag there were food scraps scattered around. He thought maybe this was by the eagles or by whoever had owned it, perhaps they had stopped to eat. He said at least once a year a person will jump from these cliffs and take their life. It's seen as a noble way to go if you live in these parts and must commit suicide for whatever reason, but no one would ever jump from this particular point because of the ledge below, which would stop you from falling all the way to the sea, which is what happened with you. He said, if he were a detective, he would have decided that you stopped to eat lunch, and maybe the wind picked up, and as you were trying to pack your belongings a gust of wind set you off balance and you tumbled backwards before you could reach for this rope. This rope, he said, he installed himself, as there have been many other accidents on this pass over the years. You are lucky to survive, many who've been unlucky enough to get caught in storms up here have vanished.'

'So it wasn't suicide then,' I said.

'It wasn't suicide, Artie, and I need you to believe this now.'

'I believe it,' I decided, 'I need to believe it.'

'If you want to keep on living then yes, you do.'

'I want to keep on living, Emilio.'

'Good, but there are many ways to kill yourself Artie, a jump off a cliff is one, staring down an empty bottle is another.'

I walked over to Fonsu and put out my hand for him to shake, instead he pulled me close and gave me a giant hug, his ancient face settling into my chest.

'*Muchas gracias*,' I said.

'*De nada*,' he responded, smiling. '*De nada, de nada, de nada*.' Then he led us back the way we came, Cantabrian eagles always circling overhead, checking to see if and when we were ready to die.

23

On the morning of the film festival, looking like a sailor lost at sea and presumed drowned, Tito came back in to my life. He charged into my apartment as I was eating breakfast on the couch. His hair was a knotted mess and his shirt was open to the waist, buttons missing and stained with red wine. He wore two socks but only one shoe and had more facial hair than I'd ever seen him wear before. Around his eyes were two dark, charcoal circles, heavy with regret.

'Artie, I've been trying to call, what the hell happened to the phone?' he asked as he walked over to where it used to be.

'Forget about the phone, what the hell happened to you?'

'We'll have to get this fixed,' he said, fingering the hole in the wall. 'Tony might be a drunk but he's a drunk who cares about his stuff.'

'You're the one who needs fixing, *Tio*, what the hell have you been up to?'

'I eloped,' he said, shrugging his shoulders as if eloping were the most natural thing in the world. 'I had no choice, the sea was calling.'

'And where exactly did you elope to?' I asked.

'Oh I don't know, Barcelona, Ibiza, other places. I woke up this morning on a fishing boat in the Ionian Sea, a half mile off Cephalonia. I had to charter a jet to get back in time for tonight. It cost me a fortune Artie!'

'Who were you with?'

'This morning? I don't know their names, but they swore that they were sisters.'

'No, who did you elope with?'

'Oh, right. The daughter of a Russian oligarch who's had a thing for me ever since her father financed one of my films when she was just a kid. I lost her somewhere in the south of France, somewhere between Montpellier and Monaco. Look, Artie, I need your help.'

'You need more than my help, *Tio*, you are a job for professionals, a team of them.'

'Maybe, but I don't trust doctors, Artie, haven't been to one in fifteen years. Look, let's start with a drink,' he said as he entered the kitchen, 'and we'll go from there.'

'I'm good,' I called out after him, 'just get yourself one.'

He came back into the living room with a cross between suspicion and disbelief on his face. 'Artie, are you ok?' he asked.

'I'm fine, why?'

'If you're dying you need to tell me, it'll mean another speech and I won't be happy at all.'

'What? Why do you think I'm dying?'

'You just turned down a drink.'

'Oh right, yeah, it's a new thing I'm trying. I made a promise to Emilio, I'd try and cut down a little.'

'I knew that man was a bad influence,' he said, returning to the couch with a scotch on the rocks.

'So, what was the purpose of this elopement?' I asked. 'And thanks for telling me.'

'I'm sorry, Artie, I would've told you, but I was high, and it didn't occur to me and then I stayed high until this morning when I paddled back to shore with the sisters, the younger one doing most the work. I've been afraid, that's all, I needed to escape.'

'I understand,' I said, 'it's normal I suppose, happens to everyone. Although the manner in which you did it probably isn't normal but then again not everyone is a millionaire film producer.'

'Exactly, Artie, and if they were they'd do it in precisely the same way, it was brilliant.'

'Do anything you regret?'

'Apart from returning here? *Nada!*'

'Are you ready for tonight?' I asked.

'God no, not at all, are you?'

'I can't go, no chance, absolutely not. I haven't got anything to wear, anyway. Emilio and I assumed you'd either fled for good or were dead in a ditch, so I didn't bother going shopping.'

'Is that so? Did you call the police at least?'

'There's no phone,' I shrugged.

'Fair enough. Look I have plenty of suits, Artie, we'll get you looking sharp. I have a ticket for Coco too.'

'Ah, we definitely won't be needing that.'

'Why, what happened?'

'Coco left, the day after I last saw you, she's gone to live with Javier, at least I think that's where she is.'

'Oh Artie,' he said, putting his arm around me, 'I'm really sorry about that.'

'It's ok,' I replied, 'I've made peace with it.'

'You're over her then?' he asked.

'No, I probably never will to be honest, but I've accepted that Coco isn't interested.'

'Well, I dare say you'll see her tonight if you want to smooth things over. Javi never misses these events.'

'I really would rather just stay at home, *Tio*, that sounds like hell.'

'You can't, Artie, I need you in my corner tonight, and god knows I've given you enough cash these last two months to have afforded at least this. Don't worry about Javi, when it comes down to it, he doesn't have much of a backbone. I'm sure Coco will be back here before the night is through.'

'You know something Tito, you're a wonderful uncle but a fucking terrible father,' I said.

'A terrible son deserves a terrible father I suppose, I'm just playing my part.'

'You play it well.'

We spent the rest of the morning and the early afternoon working on something that resembled a speech. It was fairly short and rambled on incoherently before thanking everyone in the room and then abruptly ending. It confirmed to Tito and me that while we may want to be inspired, creative types, we weren't, not at all. That was best left to people like Emilio and Coco, who felt their way through life, saw the beauty and nuance in everything, noticed things like nautilus spirals and got them tattooed on their necks, rather than brutes like Tito and me who charge right on through life while never glancing sideways. And while we loved their types and needed them around us we could never be them. And who knows, maybe they needed us too? One thing we did do well, however, was have a good time, and despite the promise I'd made Emilio, I figured a few drinks wouldn't go astray. At least these ones were social, and I wasn't drinking alone for a change.

Tito and I stood in front of the mirror with matching tuxedos, greying facial hair and half-drunk martinis, looking like a couple of washed-up relics from the Riviera set of the 1920s.

'We look absurd,' he said, gulping down the rest of his drink, 'but utterly fuckable.'

'Maybe you do; my leg might be a turn-off though.' We had managed to hide the cast under the suit pants, which made it bulge to twice the size of the other.

'Just keep your crutches handy and no one will think anything of it.'

'Well, if I want to walk I won't have a choice.'

'You know, I could be your father, Artie.'

'You ever sleep with my mother?'

'I don't think so.'

'Then you're probably not my father.'

'You think Javi looks like me?' he asked.

I studied him in the reflection, 'Not at all, to be honest, he's a lot thinner, taller, a completely different body type.'

'I agree. I was thinking just this morning as the sisters paddled me to shore—his mother was a bit of a whore, as was I, we both slept around a lot back then, and maybe he isn't actually mine.'

'That'd save you some money at least.'

'And embarrassment. I'm starting to think he's actually involved in ETA.'

'What makes you say that?'

'Just a comment he made before the bombs in Malaga the other week. I have no proof, it's just a hunch.'

'Maybe you should tell the police, an anonymous tip perhaps?'

'I can't do that, they'd lock him up without trial and he's probably innocent. Spain might have rid itself of Franco but the Guardia Civil still exist, and you don't mess with the Guardia Civil.'

'Fair enough,' I said, finishing my drink.

'Shall we do a line of coke,' he asked, as casually as suggesting a morning coffee.

'No, not for me, I'm off it. And is it such a good idea? You'll be on stage in a few hours.'

'Good point, Artie,' he said, 'I'm well behind schedule, I'll have to do two.'

24

The opening night was at the Kursaal Palace, which was the official name of the opera house which sat between Tito's apartment and my own. We spent the early evening relaxing on his balcony, watching the limousines arrive as celebrities paraded down the red carpet, which was actually a shade of pink and not red. Tito was on his feet trying to pick out celebrities he knew in the crowd.

'Shame your telescope isn't here, Artie, my eyes aren't what they used to be.'

'Fuck that telescope,' I said, 'it caused me way more trouble than it was worth.'

'Without that telescope you wouldn't have found Coco,' he said.

'True, and without it I wouldn't have lost her.'

He stood up and leant over the balcony, trying to

focus his eyes. 'I think that's Antonio, yes that's definitely Antonio. And that's Melanie. I was supposed to
have lunch with them today, I completely forgot. I'll
have to spend the night avoiding them.'

'Just invite them back here after, I'm sure they'll
forgive and forget.'

'Oh, everyone comes back here after, Artie, you
and I might have a hard time getting in ourselves,' he
said, downing the last of his whiskey. 'OK, we really
should head over, you ready?' he asked.

'Ready,' I responded, collecting my crutches.

'I have to admit though, Artie, I'm feeling pretty
nervous. How do I look?'

'Like you woke up on a fishing boat off the coast of
Cephalonia.'

'Good,' he said, 'it's my personal brand and it
hasn't failed me yet, let's go.'

As we approached the pink carpet the entire place
erupted. Tito was by far one of the most loved and
respected celebrities attending the festival. I was quickly
pushed aside as photographers, fans, interviewers and
movie stars swarmed all over him, asking him to pose
for photos, sign autographs, or hoping to steal a kiss.
A thin, wormish looking man with big black-rimmed
glasses and a pencil moustache pulled Tito out of
the scrum and handed him two passes. They started
speaking in Spanish before Tito asked him to switch to
English for my sake.

'I am very sorry, my English is not so good.'

'I'm the one who should be sorry,' I responded.

'Very well,' he said. 'There is a room at the back

for you, *Señor Ramirez*. If you can be there in two hours I will get you for your award. Room number…' he checked his clipboard, '…fifteen. Did I say that right? Fifteen?'

'Fifteen is good,' I said.

'Thank you, it is a big honour to meet you both.'

'Likewise,' I replied, somewhat awkwardly, as I shook his tiny, reptilian hand. Then Tito was yanked away by an interviewer from an online magazine.

'Artie, take this,' he said as he slipped me my entry pass, 'go enjoy the bar or try and meet a nice girl, just drop my name and it shouldn't be too hard.' I took the pass and slid out anonymously into the hall.

I was barely afforded a sideways glance as I limped through the crowds of the rich and famous and the leeches of the rich and famous, those desperate to get something off them, anything off them, even an STI was a prize. I guessed it was split fairly evenly at fifty-fifty. There were the failed actors, having paid a small fortune for the privilege of attending an event where they weren't even welcome, where they'd never be welcome, hoping to steal a moment with a Woody Allen or a Pedro Almodovar and state their case, explain, beg if they had to, how they would be a huge star if only someone gave them a chance, if only someone rec-ognised just how talented they were, if only someone had the balls to take a risk on them. In reality they were failed actors for a reason and that's all they'd ever be, but reality wasn't something they were interested in, not tonight anyhow. Then there were the Russian models, quite possibly underage, with badly forged documents to suggest otherwise, hanging off the arms of multimillionaire movie-moguls who plied them with cocaine for sloppy blowjobs in elevators. Their eyes were half-way to vacant already, like a newborn lamb not yet led to slaughter, not quite old enough to understand that this was as good as it was ever going to be. Amongst all this rabble there were the odd legitimates though, genuine producers, who were by far the worst dressed and the least charismatic in the room, the ones with the least interesting stories but the ones holding all the power. They were the top of the food chain but the masters of camouflage. They'd decide which, if any, of the films pitched over the next two weeks would ever see the light of day. They'd pull strings to decide which directors were rewarded long careers and which were thrown on the scrap-heap of one-hit wonders. They'd be the ones to decide which actors were lucky enough to stop waiting tables and which were doomed to a lifetime of community theatre knock-backs. They weren't interested in the cheap sex or the free drugs or the after parties that kicked on till dawn, they were only interested in building up their CVs, for the ones with the flashiest CV would be able to afford the biggest vineyard in the Tuscan Hills. The directors, movie stars and socialites were just cannon-fodder for the rest, cheap carrion for cheap scavengers. There were some amongst them who cared about the art, but they numbered about one in a hundred. This was a place to get laid, fill your nose with Colombia's finest and line your pockets with cold hard cash, mostly illegal, which made sense as to why my uncle Tito was their king.

I moved through the corridors like a ghost, paying no attention to anyone and being paid none back. I found a bar with an empty stool and decided to pass the time there until Tito would be called to stage. I ordered a whiskey and made myself comfortable. It wasn't long before there was a tap on my shoulder. I swung around on my stool and lost all my words.

'Artie, you look great,' she said, leaning in to hug me, 'how are you?'

'I…' was all I said, what the hell was I supposed to say? Tito had warned me I'd most likely see her, but I didn't believe it'd actually happen, I didn't want to get my hopes up, I'd meditated on the idea all day that she wouldn't be here.

'Are you ok?' she asked.

I looked at my glass and finished what was left. I signalled to the bartender for another, I was going to need it.

'Hi Coco,' I managed, after what must have seemed an eternity.

She wore a long black dress, loose at the top and flowing to her feet, it was similar to the one she wore the afternoon we met in the bar during the storm. Her hair was pulled back, displaying long silver earrings, which spun around themselves in the shape of a nautilus spiral. In the middle were diamonds. Her makeup was dark, especially around her eyes, much darker than I'd ever seen it before, as if she were hiding something, hiding everything.

'You look different,' I said, as I reached for the fresh drink, 'different to how I remember you.'

'Good or bad different?' she asked, nervous to get an answer.

'Good, I suppose, but older,' I said.

She laughed, 'You look older too with that huge beard, and so many white hairs,' she touched my face.

'You gave me these,' I responded, moving her hand away, 'they're your legacy.'

'It's a nice legacy, they suit you. Have you been well?' she asked.

'Well enough,' I lied. 'And you?'

'I've been ok,' she said, glancing up at me, her eyes secretly confessing that she'd been anything but ok, far from it. 'I was really hoping I'd see you tonight.'

'You were?'

'Yes, I really need to talk to you, it's important.'

'I'm not sure that's a good idea,' I said. 'My cousin doesn't look too happy.'

I nodded in the direction of the doorway, where Javier was standing. Just standing there and staring at us intensely. Coco turned to look but quickly turned back. I decided in this moment that my uncle was correct, Javier was almost certainly a psychopath, and as luck would have it, Coco and I were likely going to be his victims.

'Artie, promise me tonight we can talk, it's important,' she said, almost whispering, her voice collapsing to a stammer.

'I find that strange Coco, I wasn't important to you two weeks ago.'

'Don't say things like that, you've always been important to me, don't act like all this is my fault, it's not fair. I'm going back to Javi now, it's for the best, but later, at your uncle's place, can we talk?'

'I'll think about it.'

'Just say yes, Artie.'

'Ok, yes.'

'Thank you,' she leant in and kissed me on the cheek. 'You have no idea how much I've missed you.'

She backed away, holding eye contact for longer than she ought to, and then turned and rejoined him. He leaned down and whispered into her ear, spitting venom like a cut snake, still staring sharply in my direction. I swung around and noticed my drink was empty and so I called the waiter over.

'Just keep them coming if you can, it's one of those nights.'

25

About an hour or two later, and however many drinks that meant, the wormish little guy with the glasses came and grabbed me by the shoulders and swung me round, damn near throwing me off my comfortable little stool.

'I've been looking everywhere for you,' he yelped. 'You need to help me with Tito!' He was sweating profusely and looked utterly defeated, like he'd just run last in a marathon he was expected to win.

'Why?' I asked, now well on my way to drunken bliss, 'why does Tito need help? He's a big boy, you've seen the size of him, he's huge.'

'He is a small boy, a baby boy, you know this! A very, very tiny baby boy! Just follow me.'

'I don't want to.'

'Well, too bad!'

I tried to pay but the little guy yanked at me and gestured something to the bartender along the lines of 'It's on me, I'll fix it later' and we bailed together like we were storming out of a burning building. He led me through the hordes of sinners and sinned against and took me through a curtain guarded by a security guy with shoulders twice as wide as he was tall and a face like an elephant's backside.

'Where the hell are you taking me?' I asked, trying to pull free of his grip on my upper arm. 'I was happy at the bar.' He gripped me tighter.

'I'm not surprised,' he quipped, 'you are your uncle's nephew after all.'

'I thought you couldn't speak English?' I asked.

'I couldn't, but I'm learning on the job.'

He brought me to a door numbered 15. We tried to open it, but it was locked from the inside.

'He's your uncle, do something!' the little punk commanded.

'What the hell do you want me to do? You want me to kick it down?' I asked.

'I don't care, all I know is Meryl Streep is on stage improvising until he comes out, and she isn't happy about it.'

'Improvising eh, your English is improving by the second.'

'Open it!' he shouted.

'Fucking Meryl Streep!' I whispered under my breath. I'd never even seen a film of hers and now I was at her goddamn mercy. I bashed at the door like a landlord whose rent was three months overdue.

'Tito! It's Artie! Open up!' There was no response. I tried again, a different tone perhaps, although I was too drunk to know. 'Tito, please open the door, there's a strange little dude jabbing me in the ribs and I really want to go home or at least back to the bar so please open!' Nothing. I went to knock again and then I heard something from the other side. The door opened.

'Go away, Artie,' Tito said, 'I don't feel too well.' He tried to close the door on me but I forced my way in.

'Tito, what's up, why can't you go onstage?'

He said nothing. Instead he half-collapsed onto the table behind him, which was coated in a fine haze of clumsily snorted cocaine. I counted three empty bags on the table.

'Tito, I'm going to call an ambulance,' I said, trying to get him to relax on the couch, 'you've gone way too far tonight. Way too far.'

'Artie, no, the scandal will be too big, no ambulance.'

'Give me your phone,' I demanded.

'Not in a million years.'

'Tito, please?'

He shook his head and so I jumped on him on the couch, trying to wrestle his phone away from his pocket. Despite his state he quickly overpowered me and had me by the neck. I'd forgotten that all his years as an actor had introduced him to several forms of martial arts. Tito was not a man easily overpowered.

'Artie, listen to me, go on stage, collect the award. I'll call Emilio, I'll see you tomorrow.'

'You promise?'

'I promise, now go!'

'Alright,' I squeaked beneath his grip, 'but you'll have to release me first.'

He let me free and I waited until he was on call to Emilio, then I quit the room and turned to the tiny worm guy in the corridor, 'He doesn't want to come out, just cancel the award, he doesn't deserve it anyway.'

'No, no, no, no, no,' he said, waving his arms like a lunatic, 'No!' He grabbed me by the arm again and led me up the hallway, past the make-up rooms and the guys raising curtains and pointing TV cameras and thrust me towards the stage.

'If your uncle can't accept the award, then you will do it for him!'

He pushed me in the chest and I staggered out backwards, almost collapsing onto my crutch as I turned around and faced the audience, all five thousand of them clapping wildly despite the fact they had no idea who the hell I was or why I was up there in front of them. I was blinded by the lights above me and turned to my right where I could just make out Meryl Streep, grasping at the air like an idiot, probably just as perplexed as I was and probably just as afraid. I walked slowly towards her as she reached out her hand and gripped mine, she pulled me to the microphone.

'Hi… you,' she said, having no idea who I was. She beckoned for me to speak, almost begged me to do so.

'Hi,' I said into the microphone and then I paused as I hadn't anything else to add. The place erupted into a mix of applause and laughter, figuring it was some kind of poorly rehearsed skit. Whatever the hell was going on it was good enough for them, it was just the right amount of weird. 'I don't know you and you don't know me,' I continued, 'but I'm here tonight to apologise for my uncle, Tito Ramiro Ramirez, who can't make it because he's stuck backstage… stuck backstage with something more important to do. You all know what it is, I suppose, and I'm sorry, but he is very thankful that you recognised him tonight, and he loves you all very much. '

I turned to Meryl, who handed me a statue, which looked like something between an angel and a loaf of bread. Then I paused and turned back to the microphone.

'Actually,' I went on, 'actually my uncle is sick. He is sick from a lifestyle, a lifestyle that this industry has not only supported but enabled. Without all of you, all you frauds and fakers, he might be a decent man, maybe he'd marry Cecilia, who is here tonight, I think. Cecilia, if you're out there, can you let out a yell?' I paused and waited for Cecilia to respond. Instead there was nothing, just a few boos from the back of the auditorium, which were getting louder the longer I paused. 'Ok, maybe she's not here, but the point I'm trying to make is …'

Before I could finish two security guards came and gripped me on either side and pulled me away from the microphone, almost knocking me over as they did so. They led me past Meryl, who was shaking her head in disgust, and tossed me out the back exit of the building. Somewhere along the way I had dropped the statue but I didn't bother trying to get it back, no one deserved it anyhow, especially not Tito. I felt like a fool, an idiot, and I was furious at my uncle for having put me in that situation. No doubt I'd be all over the papers tomorrow and I felt like quitting San Sebastian once and for all. I looked up and saw the lights of my apartment and hurried back there as quickly as possible, desperately wanting to hide myself from the world.

I approached my building and as I was putting the key into the lock an enormous blow cracked across the back of my skull and I fell hard on the pavement. The world spun and bright colours danced around me.

26

When I came to, I was upstairs in my apartment on the couch. My vision was all but gone and my head was thumping hard and fast like an engine on its dying legs. I looked around and I could just make out a figure sitting opposite. He was wearing a dark suit, but my eyesight was too far gone to make out much else.

'What happened down there?' I asked. There was a silence, a long malignant silence. 'Is that you Tito? You really fucked up tonight,' I muttered through bleeding gums, 'you made me look like a fucking fool.'

'I'm not Tito, and the why fuck can you still not speak Spanish?' the figure sneered.

'Javier? You piece of shit, what have you done to me?'

'No less than you deserved, primo.'

I tried to get to my feet, but my leg was aching bad

and Javier jabbed me back down in the couch using one of my own crutches. I collapsed into myself as the buzzer of the apartment rang.

'I wonder who that could be,' Javier said as he got to his feet. My eyes had cleared up a little now and I could make out blood all over the front of his suit. He must have carried me up all those stairs I guessed, he was even stronger than I gave him credit. I touched the back of my head and it was soaking wet. I looked at my hand—the red of a massacre. The buzz happened again.

Javier didn't bother speaking into the intercom, instead he just let up whoever it was downstairs and waited for them by the door. I figured it'd be either Coco or Emilio and I was desperately hoping it was Emilio as I didn't know what good, if any, Coco could do. The door swung open and Javier stood to hide himself behind it. Coco burst into the apartment, her black eye makeup now streaming down her face, revealing bruised eye sockets.

'Oh my god, Artie,' she said through a torrent of tears as she moved towards me, 'what did he do to you?'

As she entered the living room she let the door close on itself and Javier moved behind her, unseen like a stalking beast. I tried to warn her but I was too weak to raise my arms and my voice was still barely audible.

'Coco,' I stammered, trying to point, 'behind…'

Before she could turn around Javier had gripped her by the neck and threw her onto the opposite couch.

'You little bitch!' he snapped as he slapped her across the face, 'you tell me he means nothing to you and then you cry these tears for him.' He slapped her again.

I managed to get myself onto my feet and lunged myself at him, wrapping my arms around his throat, trying to wrestle him onto the ground. He elbowed me in the ribs and overpowered me quickly and easily, then smashed me across the jaw with a fierce right hook. I spun around and collapsed onto the floor in a lifeless mess. I felt him grab my shoulder and spin me onto my back, then he lowered himself down and straddled me, pinning my arms to the ground in one swift motion. I heard something in my leg crack as he put all his weight on me, and then he brought his massive head down and smashed it into mine. Everything went colourful again as the pools of blood filled my eye sockets and my vision faded once and for all.

'Artie, dear cousin,' his mouth close down next to my ear, his warm breath, smelling of rum and mint, sticking to my skin, 'you think it's wise to tell people I'm a terrorist? You don't think Coco the little bitch tells me everything? You made the mistake of trusting her Artie, and she never gave a fuck about you, she told me as much, and then you told her I was a terrorist. This is how rumours spread and people go to jail or get shot. Is that what you wanted? You wanted me to disappear, then you could have my father and all his money to yourself? You're a smart boy Artie, but you made the mistake of trusting a whore.' He head-butted me again, although not as violently this time, I gathered he was losing strength too. Then he leaned in even closer, and I could just discern some movement behind him. 'The saddest thing for you Artie, is maybe you were right, maybe I am a terrorist, but unfortunately for you, you won't be around to find out.'

Javier leaned back and raised his right arm, his hand forming into a brick-sized fist, which he was about to finish me off with, a fatal blow no doubt. I was too weak to resist anymore and braced myself for the worst. I'd had a good run I figured, I'd seen a bunch of places, I'd definitely had my share of fun, although I was pissed off as hell this violent thug would escape to cause more carnage. I closed my eyes and then heard a brutal crack like a car crash, the sound of glass and bone smashing all at once intermingled into a horrific noise that was almost deafening, accompanied by a piercing shriek that sounded like the life being sucked out of a giant carnivore. Then I felt the enormous weight of Javier's body fall away from me and collapse in a pile to my right. I remained perfectly still, too afraid to move, too spent to breath, too delirious to care. I opened my eyes slowly, anticipating another blow, and through the blood I could just make out Coco, her own face smashed up and bleeding, standing tall above me with a glistening brass object in her hand. It was the telescope, and it was now bent at a right angle in the middle. I looked to my right and Javier lay motionless, the right side of his head leaking brains onto the carpet. Coco dropped the murder weapon and crawled down to my level.

'Artie, oh Artie,' she whispered, 'what have I done?'

'Coco,' I stammered, 'you need to leave. Call an ambulance and leave.'

'I can't leave you, what if he wakes up? What if you bleed to death?'

I looked at Javier once more. 'He's dead, Coco, he isn't gonna wake up, and they'll come looking for you. It doesn't matter what he's done, they're going to want you.'

Her sobbing became almost uncontrollable as she cradled my head and wiped the blood from my eyes. She kissed me, my own blood mixing with her saliva, 'Artie,' she said, 'where can I go? I have no-one, nothing.'

'You'll think of something.'

'But I can't leave you.'

'You've gotta leave me, Coco, they'll lock you up otherwise, you're already on the run.'

She kissed me again, 'Did you ever love me, Artie?'

'Sure did. And you?'

'Since the day we met,' she stopped crying and sat up a little. She looked over at Javier. 'I'm sorry about him, I'm sorry I went with him at all, I didn't want to hurt you so I thought I had to leave you. I was so dumb.'

'I was dumb too, I was always dumb.'

'And I shouldn't have said anything about terrorism, we were high, we were high the whole time, every minute we were high. I shouldn't have said it.'

I could hear commotion in the staircase outside the apartment now, we'd obviously disturbed a few neighbours during the scuffle and it wouldn't be long until the cops were at the door.

'Coco, you're running out of time, the police will be here soon, you've got to run.'

'I'll call an ambulance,' she said.

'It's too late, just go.'

'How will you find me though, Artie?'

'I'll look for the spirals, I'll just keep searching for the spirals.'

She kissed me once more, and the last thing she said to me was 'I'm sorry,' which was also the first thing she'd ever said to me. Then she got up and ran out of the apartment, causing a stir with the neighbours who'd gathered around the door. I closed my eyes and there was a bright shining light pulsating furiously, and then very quickly everything went black, a cool and calm black, peaceful even, like a still and generous sea under a midnight summer sky. The sea spun in a nautilus spiral and it sucked me downwards and I was happy to disappear into it, happy to disappear into Coco. Suddenly the pain went away and I had no more thoughts, thoughts were beyond me now, thoughts were for the living.

27

I woke up to a blinding light. There were figures moving over me like shadow puppets in a play. They were speaking Spanish and I could understand about half their words. My face hurt like no pain I'd ever experienced before and I tried to move my jaw to speak but it was as if the thrust of a knife shot through my skull and I let out a yell. Someone moved beside me and injected a purple fluid into a pipe fixed in my arm and I began to relax. The pain faded into nothingness and a calm overtook me. I closed my eyes and slept comfortably, peacefully even.

The next time I woke up I didn't hurt so much. A soft afternoon light flooded into the room and I was finally able to understand where I was, back in the same hospital as last time, although in a completely different room now. A fat nurse with her hair pulled back fussed around me as she fiddled with the machine I was hooked up to.

'Can I have some water?' I asked. She threw me a stunned look, as if I'd just insulted her. '*Agua*,' I said, '*agua, por favor*.'

'*Si*,' she nodded, her flabby chin wobbling where a jaw might be, and left the room. A moment later she returned with a glass of water and Dr. Rodriguez, who was either having a stressful day or was none too happy to see me, probably both.

'Hi, doctor,' I said, my jaw barely opening, 'nice to see you.'

'Really?' she asked, raising an eyebrow behind her tortoise-shell glasses. 'It's nice to see me?' I didn't know how to respond so I just offered her a dumb smile, hoping to disarm her a little. 'I don't think it's nice to see you Arthur, not at all, you'll have to excuse my honesty.'

'Oh,' I said, 'that's too bad.'

'What sort of life were you living in that apartment? We all agreed that having a live-in nurse would guarantee a safe and speedy recovery for you but it seems to have done just the opposite. You won't be surprised to learn that Emilio will no longer be nursing here.'

'Why's that?'

'Why do you think? The alcohol level in your blood was enough to kill most people, we found traces of cocaine in your system and you'd been putting un-manageable levels of stress on your leg, it's amazing it's healed at all. Not to mention your cousin was found with a caved-in skull in your living room, fighting for his life.'

'A caved-in skull?' I asked.

Her features softened for a moment as she shifted on her feet. She broke eye contact and looked down, 'I suppose you haven't been told yet. Javier was very badly wounded, he almost drowned in a pool of blood next to you. A young woman was seen running from the apartment, also bleeding. The police have a lot of questions for you.'

'So he's not dead?'

'No, he should recover in time but he'll never be the same. Anyway, I'll arrange for the police to come by tomorrow, assuming you feel well enough.'

'I feel fine,' I said, 'and sorry doctor, it all got a little of out hand.'

'You're telling me.' She went to leave the room but I interrupted her.

'Sorry, doctor, do you know if the police caught the girl?'

'You'll have to ask them yourself, Arthur.'

That evening there were no visitors, no Tito, no Emilio. I wondered if they knew where I was and what had happened. I was still angry at Tito for that episode at the ceremony. I wondered how Tito was managing with both his son and nephew in a hospital after a brutal fight. I thought I should be glad that Javier was still alive, but I disturbed myself when I realised I was actually disappointed. After the way he had smacked Coco around I wished he had died, I wished that the telescope had taken his whole head off. I thought about climbing out of bed, slipping into his room, and suf-focating him with a pillow. Or better yet blowing him up, it was his preferred modus operandi after all. Of course, though, I did nothing, I just remained where I was and stared at the ceiling and let my thoughts spiral into madness. Had Coco gotten away? That's what concerned me the most. Where would she have gone? Maybe to the village in the mountains, although I doubted it, that seemed too obvious an escape. I figured I'd know nothing until I spoke with the police tomorrow, so I tried to calm my mind and sleep. It turned out to be impossible, though, and when the sun rose the next morning, I hadn't slept a minute. My jaw hurt, my head hurt, my everything hurt. The cops turned out to be a real couple of assholes, too.

'Full name?' said the older one, an American with a booming southern voice who was representing Interpol, or so he said. He had a huge gut, which was bursting out of his trousers, and a dirty old moustache which he sucked on while concentrating. The other one, a wiry Spanish guy with a fixed stare and a slicked-back hairdo said nothing, he just scribbled notes on a pad.

'Arthur Washington.'

'Where are you from?'

'Sydney, Australia.'

'How long have you been in Spain?'

'Since late May I suppose.'

'What visa are you on?' he asked, the wiry guy scribbling down everything.

'I don't have a visa, I don't need one, I've got two passports, Australian and Spanish.'

'How did you manage that?' he asked, hardening his gaze.

'My father was born here and he organised a passport for me. I renew it every five years.'

'It is illegal here in Spain,' said the Spanish cop, pulling himself away from his notepad, 'to have two citizenships.'

'I wasn't aware,' I said, 'no-one told me that before.'

'What happened on the night of the 18th of September?'

'You want the whole night or just the end of it, in the apartment?'

'Start at the beginning,' he said.

I told them that Tito and I had started drinking during the day, that we watched the guests arrive from the balcony, that Tito was too ill to accept his award and so I did it for him and made a real ass of myself. I told them on the way back to the apartment Javier had blindsided me and carried me up the four flights of stairs. I told them that Coco had arrived and that Javier attacked her, which caused a scuffle between him and I. I told them that Javier quickly overpowered me and that Coco saved my life by hitting him with the telescope. I told them she didn't mean to kill him—she was just trying to save me. I told them that Javier had confessed to being a terrorist and I assumed he was working with ETA, although apart from this confession I had no evidence. Everything up to that point was the truth.

The skinny cop wrote it all down, seemingly word for word. The American cop just sat there and listened, never taking his eyes off me. I could see the gears turning in his mind, I could see that he'd already decided that he didn't like me one bit and he was going to make this as hard for me as possible.

'Tell us more about this Coco character,' he said, sucking on that damn moustache again.

'Well,' I started, 'I met her several weeks ago, maybe a few months, and after a while we started a relationship. It didn't work out though and then she left me for my cousin Javier, for whatever reason, she never said.'

'Was Coco her real name?'

'She never told me, I think it might have been fake.'

'Is this her?' he asked, handing me a security photo of Coco in an airport. Her hair was pulled back tight and she had a black backpack on.

'That's her, yes,' I said.

'Did she ever mention anything about her past?'

'No, nothing, she was very secretive, she'd make jokes every now and then but they were all lies. At least I think they were all lies.'

'Would it surprise you, Arthur,' the cop straightened himself a little, his back getting tired from supporting his gigantic, American gut, 'if I told you this girl was actually a Belgian criminal named Sofia who is wanted for her assistance with a diamond smuggling ring?'

'That would surprise me, yes, of course it would surprise me,' I replied, although in actuality it didn't surprise me at all, it all made sense somehow, the comments about Julia's earrings, her own earrings at the ceremony, the unease that crippled her whenever someone brought up her past. It made perfect sense, but I couldn't let them know that.

'Why of course?'

'Well it's not every day you find out a former lover is being hunted down by Interpol for smuggling diamonds. How could it not be surprising?'

'Where is she now?' he asked, leaning forward. 'We know you know. It's a real feather in my cap if I catch a Pink Panther and I'm not about to let you rest until you give her up. I want the exact fucking coordinates!'

'I have no idea.'

'Bullshit, Arthur. Let me make it real clear what's at stake for you right now. Not only will we charge you with attempted murder of your cousin Javier, but we can lock your uncle Tito up for importing and exporting cocaine in and out of Spain. Why do you think he was in Greece with a Russian heiress two days ago? We know a hell of a lot more than you think. So if you want to protect yourself and your uncle you're going to have to give us Sofia, or Coco or whatever the hell you call her. How do you want to play this?'

I looked at the two of them and could tell they weren't bluffing. Even though I was confident I could get off for the attempted murder charge there was no way Tito would be let off lightly, if what they said was true that is. I had assumed for a while he'd been dealing coke and they obviously knew a hell of a lot more than I did. I figured I only had one choice.

'There's a town, it's in the Spanish Pyrenees, about five hours from here, it's called Aragües del Porto.'

The American looked to the Spaniard, who nodded to suggest he knew the place or at least had heard of it.

'Coco and I stayed in a cottage there, owned by a

friend of my uncle. I instructed her to head out there, lay low and wait for me. She promised me she would. You have to believe me though, I knew nothing about the diamond thing, if I had I probably would've given her up.'

The two officers stood up and straightened themselves out, then the American sucked up his gut and turned back to me and fixed his eyes on my own.

'If we find out you're lying to us Arthur we are going to crush you, we'll make sure both you and your uncle rot in prison like the filthy little dogs you are.' He went to leave and then stopped once more and reached into his briefcase, 'Oh, I almost forgot,' he said as he flung a newspaper at me, 'quite the family you lot are. Your cousin will never see the light of day again, but hopefully for everyone's sake you will.'

I looked at the front page, ETA had detonated a car bomb near Santander. A soldier had been killed. More bombs were expected over the coming days.

28

That evening, despite the mental and physical exhaustion of the last few months and the rollercoaster of emotion over the last few days, I managed to sleep. I was awoken around ten by someone gently squeezing my hand. I sat up disorientated and couldn't quite work out who it was, and then I recognised him.

'Emilio,' I said, unable to hide the joy in my voice. He was dressed in his nurse's uniform. 'You shouldn't be here, you've been fired you know? Or maybe you don't know. In any case—you're done.'

He gestured his finger to his lips, indicating I ought to stay silent. 'Good evening, Arthur,' he said softly, 'fancy finding you here again, we've come full circle.'

'Emilio, you have no idea how happy I am to see you.'

'You'll be even happier once I get this free for you.'

He produced some scissors and cut me out of my cast, the leg was thin and pale like the other one had been a month earlier. 'You're going to have to wait to shave this one on the boat, we don't have time right now,' he said.

'Boat, what boat?' I asked.

'You'll learn soon enough, Artie. Just do me a favour and play dumb, we've got to get you past this guard somehow, otherwise we're both finished.'

Emilio helped me out of bed and brought a wheelchair over for me. We struggled for a while but somehow managed to remain silent. I climbed in and he wheeled me out of the room, where a young police officer, handsome and exhausted, was standing guard over my ward. They had an animated conversation in Spanish, with Emilio insisting he was just taking me to the showers for a wash, before the guard finally relented and let us past, making it clear he'd be expecting us back in no more than ten minutes. Emilio gave him a smile and continued wheeling me through the corridors, occasionally pausing or pulling around corners when he heard other nurses or patients approaching. We went right past the washrooms and down to an exit which led to the car park.

'Ok,' he said, 'we make it out of here and we're free men Artie.'

I climbed out of the chair and put my arm over Emilio's shoulder, his busty frame keeping me upright as we limped over to his car, which was parked about fifty metres away. We climbed in and Emilio turned to me, his face deadly serious.

'Do me a favour Artie, keep your head down for a few minutes, if anyone decides to follow us it'll be better if they don't see you. I'll tell you when you can sit back up.' He pulled out of the parking lot and the hospital disappeared behind us. I didn't feel free yet, not even close. He sped along the road to San Sebastian for about five minutes before we heard a siren roar up behind us.

'Stay low, Artie,' he whispered, 'whatever you do stay low.'

The siren got louder and louder as it approached the car, red and blue lights danced across the dashboard like demons beckoning us to hell, as beads of sweat dripped down Emilio's arms and fell into his lap. Then, as suddenly as they had appeared, the sound and lights disappeared ahead as the car sped right on past us and vanished out of sight.

'Just an ambulance,' Emilio sighed, 'someone is watching over us tonight. You can sit up now Artie.'

I straightened up and looked out the window at the apartment blocks flashing past. We were almost in the heart of San Sebastian now. It was a demure night and not many people were around. As we began to slow down, Emilio gestured towards the back seat.

'You'll notice some clothes back there, when we pull up you'll need to get changed into them.'

'No problem,' I said, 'where are we going anyhow?'

'You'll see, you'll see.'

Emilio pulled the car right up to the port and parked it in a place hidden from streetlights and suspicious eyes. I climbed into the backseat and got myself dressed in black baggy trousers, a loose-fitting white shirt, and an oversized yellow fisherman's jacket. There was also a navy-blue beanie which I pulled down over my brow, I got out of the car and asked him how I looked.

'You look perfect,' he said, 'like you've just stepped off a trawler.'

Emilio led the way and I hobbled close behind him, a crutch under my arm, as we went away from the port and up some steps into a small, dimly lit fishermen's bar, which was empty except for a lone figure in the corner. He was lit by orange candle light and slouched over a table with a half-drunk beer within reach. I limped over to him.

'Tito,' I said, as he rose up to hug me, 'I'm so glad to see you.'

'Not half as glad as I am to see you Artie, I was worried sick.' We hugged a while longer, and then Emilio came over with three beers.

'How'd it go then?' Tito asked, sitting back down.

'It was easier than expected,' Emilio said, 'I only had to bribe the other nurses. Whoever the policeman was guarding the room was about as good at his job as Artie is at staying sober.'

'Oh, come on,' I said, 'he wasn't that bad.'

'Good, let's hope our luck holds up then, let's hope we haven't run out just yet,' Tito said.

'Where are we going?' I asked.

'You'll find out soon enough, Artie. I don't want to say anything just in case someone overhears,' he replied.

'There's no-one in here though,' I said, glancing around at the empty bar.

'Your uncle grew up in the days of Franco,' Emilio responded, 'as did I. We'll be glancing over our shoulders until the day we die.'

'Fair enough, then,' I said, taking a sip of beer. After a brief pause I brought up his son. 'I'm sorry about Javier, Tito, but it could have been worse, he's going to live at least.'

'Oh, fuck Javi,' Tito muttered as he made a dismissive gesture with his hand, 'they found bomb-making materials in his apartment, he'll never see the outside of a cell again and I'm not too upset about it.'

'Still, he is your son,' I said.

'No, Artie, he was my son, now that's you.'

'Oh no, that's not a good idea, you're a terrible father Tito.'

'And you're a terrible son. When was the last time you called your mother? Does she have any idea where the hell you are?' I shrugged, I had no idea what she knew. 'Remember, a terrible son deserves a terrible father,' he joked.

Then he looked at his phone and glanced towards Emilio who put down his beer and nodded. They both stood up.

'Well, Emilio,' Tito said, putting out his hand, 'thank you for everything.'

'Really, a handshake, that's all I get?' Emilio asked as he grabbed Tito and pulled him in for an epic hug. 'You take care of him, and yourself. And remember what you promised after that mess at the festival, no more cocaine.'

Tito laughed as he broke the hug, 'We'll see,' was all he said. Then he turned to me, 'Artie, I'll meet you outside, don't be long,' I nodded and then he left.

'You're not coming with us then?' I asked Emilio.

'I can't, Artie, I wish I could, but I'm opening a show.'

'I'm so sorry I won't be here to see it, I'm sure you'll be great.'

'Don't be sorry, without you it would never have happened in the first place.'

'You're a good friend, Emilio,' I said, 'the best I've ever had. Thank you for taking care of me, and everything else. Promise me you'll stay safe.'

'You'd better go kid,' he said, 'and don't worry about me, don't you know I'm an actor now? I'll act myself out of this mess.'

I hugged him once more and wished him luck; for the first time since I could remember a tear rolled down my cheek. Outside the bar Tito was waiting for me, leaning up against a wall and half-lit by an orange streetlight, looking more like a movie star than he ever had before. He gestured for me to follow him as we headed towards the port.

'So, are you going to tell me where we're going now?'

'We're going on a trip,' he said, 'a long trip. I'm not sure either of us will ever come back here.'

'Then we better look at her once more,' I said,

turning to face the town, 'she's beautiful isn't she.'

'The most beautiful there ever was, by far. But we've got to hurry, Artie, this place could be crawling with cops any minute now.'

We hurried along the port towards the wharves where the boats were docked in the late-night gloom. It was a quiet night and especially dark now, and it seemed our luck hadn't run out just yet. We continued along until we reached a boat. It was Cecilia's boat, Ulysses. We climbed on board and pulled the plank in behind us. Tito whistled a soft tune and a hatch lifted as Cecilia came out of the cabin and up to the deck, making a special effort to remain silent and invisible.

'Arthur,' she whispered, taking my hand and stroking the wounds on my face, 'I'm so glad you're safe.'

'I can't believe this' I said, 'you're taking a huge risk doing this.'

'The three of us weren't about to leave you behind, Artie,' she said, 'this place isn't safe for anyone anymore.'

'The three of you?' I asked.

The hatch to the cabin lifted up again and another figure came out. It was Coco. In the dark I couldn't see if her face had healed yet, healed from the bashing Javier had given her. She walked over and kissed me gently on the lips, making an effort to be soft.

'Cute outfit, fisherman,' she smiled, 'you ever caught a fish before?'

'To be honest, Sofia, no.'

'My stupid Australian,' she whispered, 'to you I'm Coco, I'll only ever be Coco.'

'But you're not Coco, Coco was everything to me, Coco was…'

And to shut me up she kissed me again, and this time I said nothing, I just kissed her back.

'We really have to go now,' Tito said, his eyes surveying the port. A couple of cars had pulled up and there were figures moving around in the dark.

'What's the plan?' I asked.

'Plan?' he scoffed, 'There's no plan, just four criminals on the run with a shitload of cash, eloping from Spain on a sailing boat in the dead of night. It's just another Tuesday, no?'

'Four criminals?' I asked, 'Surely at least Cecilia is innocent?'

Cecilia turned to me and raised an eyebrow, 'You have to be joking Arthur, you honestly believed Max and his lover just magically drowned? You Australians are a gullible lot.'

I couldn't help but laugh. Everything about the situation was messed up, but what else was I supposed to do? Laughing was my only escape. Cecilia straightened up the boat and led it away from port. We sailed out past the island, the headland, the continent, the whole damn lot.

Coco tugged at my arm and pointed towards the sky. 'Look,' she said.

'It better not be another of your spiral things,' I joked, as I turned to where she pointed. Yet sure enough, as clear as the crystal night itself, was a nautilus spiral formed out of stars, glittering like the fire in her eyes the very first time we met. I thought of everything that had happened since that day, I thought of Emilio, I thought of his bear hands and his bald head, and hoped he'd be alright, I hoped his show would do well, I hoped he would find happiness, and then Coco pulled me in tight and there were no more thoughts, no more hopes, nothing. Just paradise.

She looked at me and smiled, it was the smile of a pirate, as the tired lights of Spain disappeared behind her, and we faded into the deep and dark Atlantic. Her least favourite of all the oceans.

www.ingramcontent.com/pod-product-compliance
Lightning Source LLC
Chambersburg PA
CBHW020134120726

47903CB00007B/2255